FAMOUS FIRSTS IN SPACE

FAMOUS FIRSTS IN SPACE

Edward F. Dolan

Illustrated with photographs

COBBLEHILL BOOKS   Dutton · New York

PICTURE CREDITS

Associated Press, 13, 18; National Aeronautics and Space Administration, 28, 33, 41, 56, 60, 69, 70, 72, 85, 94, 96, 103, 104, 113, 121, 123, 127.

Library of Congress Cataloging-in-Publication Data

Dolan, Edward F., date
  Famous firsts in space / Edward F. Dolan.
    p.   cm.
  Bibliography: p.
  Includes index.
  Summary: Eight descriptions of "firsts" in space including first space walks, first men on the moon, and first American space shuttles.
  ISBN 0-525-65007-5
  1. Astronautics—History—Juvenile literature. 2. Manned space flight—History—Juvenile literature. [1. Astronautics—History. 2. Manned space flight—History.]   I. Title.
TL793.D57 1989
629.4'09—dc19   89-811
                                                          CIP   AC

Published in the United States by E.P. Dutton,
New York, N. Y., a division of Penguin Books USA Inc.
Published simultaneously in Canada by
Fitzhenry & Whiteside Limited, Toronto

Printed in the U.S.A.
First Edition   10 9 8 7 6 5 4 3 2 1

CONTENTS

INTRODUCTION

This book tells the stories of the first manned flights into space—flights that carried human beings into a vast unknown. They are among the greatest adventure stories of all time. They are filled with excitement and danger. They tell of courageous men and women who risked their lives to explore a new and mysterious frontier.

Manned flights make up only a part of the story of space. Another part concerns unmanned flights. These flights have been of two types. They have taken either artificial satellites or space probes aloft.

Artificial satellites are objects that man has placed in orbit around the earth. They circle the world endlessly and perform a number of tasks, such as supplying us with weather information. Probes fly deep into space and send back information about the planets and the stars.

Unmanned space flights tell an exciting story. But the stories here concentrate on the manned flights, with all their marvelous adventure—the first times that humans successfully invaded the world of space.

And so, are you ready for that adventure? Then let's get to our stories. They begin more than thirty years ago in the Soviet Union.

1.

THE FIRST STEPS INTO SPACE

The day was Friday, October 4, 1957. A strange beeping sound reached the earth. It came from a battery-operated radio. The radio was inside a metal ball that scientists in the Soviet Union had shot aloft early that morning. The ball was now several hundred miles above the earth. It was circling the world at a speed of about 18,000 miles an hour.

Known as an artificial satellite, it was the first man-made object ever to be placed in orbit around the earth. The Soviets called it *Sputnik.* In English, the word meant "fellow traveler."

SPUTNIK

Sputnik rode skyward atop a giant rocket. The two broke away from each other as they went into orbit, and the little satellite began to circle the globe by itself. "Little" was the right word for *Sputnik.* It was about the size of a basketball and weighed just 184 pounds.

Most of the weight was taken up by scientific equipment inside the satellite. As *Sputnik* raced along, the equipment gathered information and flashed it to the Soviet scientists far below. Sent down was data on the density of the atmosphere far out from earth. Also sent down were records of the temperatures there and of the cosmic rays that poured in from every side. All this information would help the scientists better understand the problems that lay ahead in space flight.

Circling the world once every 96 minutes, *Sputnik* did its job for 23 days. Then its batteries gave out. The satellite fell silent. It remained in orbit for another 70 days. It lost speed all the while and finally began to drop back to earth. Much friction was created when the satellite reached the thicker atmosphere near the earth. The friction caused the little satellite to catch fire and burn to ash.

Sputnik captured the interest of the entire world.

The flight meant one thing to everyone. The exploration of space was no longer a dream. It was becoming a reality. A new age was dawning.

A TRAVELER NAMED LAIKA

Though *Sputnik*'s journey was a major feat, a far greater challenge now faced the Soviet scientists. If space was to be fully explored, human beings had to be sent there. But the men venturing into space would face many problems.

For one, there would be pain at the start of a space journey. The pain would be caused by the increased gravity that would press in on the men when they blasted off—lifted off—in a spaceship.

Then, as they shot higher and higher, there would be less and less oxygen for them to breathe. The cabins of their spaceships would need to be pressurized and able to provide them with oxygen. The men would have to wear pressurized space suits.

And there was yet another danger. When the spaceship reached an altitude of about 100 miles, the decreasing pull of gravity and the speed of their ship would be working together to make them weightless.

Could men stand up to these many problems?

Could they take the pain at blast-off? Could they move about easily enough in space suits so that they could do their work? Could they work when weightless? Or would they fall ill? Or die? Even with the best of equipment, could they survive for long periods in space?

There were so many questions. No one knew the answers. Just one month after sending *Sputnik* aloft, the Soviet scientists went in search of some of the answers. They launched *Sputnik 2.* It carried the first living creature ever to visit space.

That traveler was not a human being. Rather, it was a dog—a female fox terrier with a spotted face and dark eyes. Her name was Laika. She weighed just 14 pounds. Her journey began on November 3, 1957.

Soviet scientists had been launching rockets with dogs on board ever since 1951. The launchings were carried out to study those terrible pressures that gravity exerted on the body at lift-off. The dogs rode in sealed containers—called capsules—and stayed aloft for just a few minutes. Then they were returned to the ground by parachute so that they could be examined.

Laika was the first to travel high enough to go into orbit around the earth. Once in orbit, the animal's capsule could not be brought home. She

The first living creature to travel in space was Laika, a female fox terrier. This picture was taken by a Soviet news photographer a few days before her historic journey.

was doomed to die when her oxygen supply ran out. It would last her but a few days. She was being sacrificed in the hope of paving the way to space for men.

Sputnik 2 weighed 1,120 pounds—more than six times as much as the first *Sputnik.* Laika traveled in a capsule perched atop a rocket that broke away as orbital height was reached. The temperature in the capsule was controlled to keep it even and comfortable. There was an ample supply of food in a special container. Another device took care of the animal's bodily wastes. Laika had just enough room to sit, stand, and lie down.

Orbiting the earth once every 103.7 minutes, Laika remained alive for a week—until November 12. Attached to her body were recording devices that sent much information back to earth. They showed that Laika did well against the pressures at lift-off—and just as well with the problem of being weightless. The little dog gave the watching scientists reason to believe that human beings could indeed work and survive in space.

The Soviets were now ready for their next space "first"—the placing of a man in orbit.

MAN IN ORBIT

While getting ready to send a man into space, the Soviets made other advances. In 1958, they fired *Sputnik 3* into orbit. It weighed about 3,000 pounds and was built to study a wide variety of subjects—from solar radiation to cosmic rays and magnetic fields. Then, in 1959, they launched three unmanned spacecraft to the moon. The ships were called Luna probes.

The first missed its target by 4,660 miles and went on toward the sun. The second crashed into the lunar surface. The third went into orbit around the moon. Cameras were housed in the circling probe. They gave the world its first photographs of the back side of the moon. It was a side never before seen by mankind.

By 1961, the Soviets were ready to launch a human being into orbit. The man selected for the journey was a 27-year-old military pilot—Senior Lieutenant Yuri A. Gagarin.

Gagarin came from a small farming village about 100 miles west of Moscow. He had always wanted to be an aviator. He had taken flying lessons while in high school and then had joined the armed forces as an aviation cadet. Throughout his training, the young man showed himself to be a fine jet pilot. In 1957, he was commissioned a lieutenant in the Soviet Air Force.

Gagarin's interest in Russia's space work equaled his love of flying. When he heard that his country was looking for its first spacemen, he applied to be one of their number. Immediately, the new officer was put through a series of difficult physical and mental tests. In one test, he was placed in a pressure chamber to see how well he stood up to the problem of being weightless.

In another, Gagarin was made to solve complex mathematical problems while a loudspeaker blared various possible answers in his ear. The test was meant to show whether he could keep on thinking clearly if his spacecraft got into trouble.

The young lieutenant passed the tests and was one of the first twelve men accepted into the Soviet space program. They were called "cosmonauts." The term "cosmo" comes from the Greek word *kosmos,* which means "universe" or "world." The United States space program uses the term "astronaut," with *astron* being the Greek word for "star." In all, cosmonaut means "traveler of the universe." Astronaut means "traveler to the stars."

The twelve cosmonauts were chosen in 1960. Barely a year later, Gagarin won the job of being the first man to travel into space and the first to orbit the earth.

THE *VOSTOK* FLIGHT

The day of Gagarin's great adventure came on April 12, 1961. Dawn was breaking when he was awakened in his quarters at the space center near the town of Tyuratum in southern Russia. After eating breakfast, he donned his orange space suit and white helmet. Then he climbed into a bus for the ride out to the launching pad. Riding with him was his fellow cosmonaut, Gherman Titov. Titov was Gagarin's backup man. If anything went wrong with Gargarin or his equipment, Titov would take his place on the flight.

But nothing went wrong. On arriving at the pad, Gagarin stepped briskly from the bus and rode the elevator up the gantry to his spacecraft. The craft bore the name *Vostok,* which means "East" in English. It sat perched atop the nose of a slender rocket. The *Vostok*'s flight cabin was some 90 feet above the ground. Far below, four large jet engines and a series of small ones circled the base of the rocket.

When Gagarin settled himself in the spacecraft, he had an hour to wait before being hurled into space. He spent the time checking his instrument panel. Television cameras had been mounted in the flight cabin. They would take pictures of the cosmonaut during the flight. Now, in the moments before lift-off, they showed him to be calm and smiling.

Lift-off came at 9:07 A.M. Moscow time. Just as the final seconds were being counted off in the

Yuri Gagarin of the Soviet Union was the first human being to travel in space. He was photographed here during a visit to England in the weeks following his orbit of the earth.

control center, Gagarin spoke into his microphone. He said, *"Vsyo normalno."* ("Everything is
normal.") Then the rocket was ignited. A roar
filled the air. Flames burst from the rocket's base.

Vostok shot skyward. Gagarin was pushed back
against his seat by the tremendous forces of gravity. He told the control center that all was well.
But, for long seconds, he could barely move his
hands and arms. He heard a sharp screaming
sound. Gagarin said it was much like the sound
of a jet plane taking off.

Performing beautifully, the rocket sent *Vostok* to
an altitude of about 200 miles and put the ship
into orbit. Then the rocket dropped away. As the
Sputniks had done, *Vostok* began to circle the earth
at a speed of 18,000 miles an hour. There was
just one difference—a great one. For the first time
in history, a man was in orbit.

At the start of its flight, *Vostok* had been covered with a metal shield to protect it against the
friction that would take shape as the ship battled
its way up through the earth's atmosphere. Once
Gagarin was in orbit, the shield fell away. Gagarin looked out the window at his side and gazed
down at the earth. He reported that he had a
breathtaking view of the sunlit side of the world.
He could make out the shores of continents and

islands. He said there was only one word to describe his feelings at that moment: joy.

As he headed into orbit, Gagarin became the first man to be weightless for more than a few seconds at a time. (Other men had been weightless in test chambers for just seconds.) He radioed that he was floating upward from his seat. The scientists in the control center listened intently, worrying that he might soon fall ill and be unable to work. But Gagarin said he was feeling fine. He was able to eat. He had no trouble checking his instrument panel and doing other jobs. He was able to write notes. There was only one problem. If not held firmly in place, his note pad kept sailing away.

Gagarin was to make one orbit. The flight was 1 hour and 18 minutes old when several small rockets in *Vostok* were fired automatically. They were retro-rockets and their job was to slow the spacecraft so that it would lose altitude and begin its return to earth.

BACK TO EARTH

Vostok faced some of its most dangerous moments when it dropped down out of orbit and entered the air of the earth's atmosphere. As usual, friction went to work and triggered a fiery heat. Gagarin saw a deep red glow as flames broke out along his ship's outer skin. Then, to make matters worse, the friction caused the spacecraft to begin tumbling along its course.

Fortunately, these problems caused Gagarin no real trouble. He told the control center that, even with the fire outside, his cabin was remaining cool. After a few moments, the flames died out and *Vostok* righted itself.

Gagarin saw the earth drawing closer with every passing second. Suddenly, the spacecraft was yanked upward. Giant parachutes had been automatically released. They gently lowered *Vostok* through the remaining moments of its journey. At last, Gagarin felt a jolt run through the ship. He was back on the ground.

His journey had taken 1 hour and 48 minutes. In that time, he had made one complete orbit of the earth and had won a lasting place in the history of space exploration.

The flight plan had called for *Vostok* to land at an air base in southwestern Russia. The spaceship, however, missed its target by a few miles and came to rest in a farm field. Because of the miss, there were no officials on hand to welcome home a man who would soon be world-famous.

Instead, two farm women ran to the *Vostok*. Wide-eyed, they watched a figure in a strange orange suit and white helmet climb out of the ship.

One of the women gathered up her courage. She stepped forward and asked the figure if he had come from space.

Gagarin smiled and said that indeed he had.

2.
THE FIRST AMERICANS IN SPACE

The United States was doing its first space work in the 1950s. But the work was moving slowly and the country was lagging far behind the Soviet Union.

In great part, this was happening because the U.S. had not put a single group in charge of its space efforts. Instead, the three armed services— the Army, the Navy, and the Air Force—were caught up in a "space race." They were working separately and trying to beat each other to the honor of being first in space.

Each service was developing its own rockets. Each was having trouble getting them off the ground. For example, the Navy once launched a rocket that traveled just five feet into the air. Then it exploded.

Many such problems might have been avoided had the three services worked together and shared information. The nation's space work might have moved ahead more quickly. But there was little or no sharing.

But then the three *Sputniks* went whirling around the earth. Americans everywhere were shocked. Their pride was deeply hurt. Their nation—the leader of the free world—was being beaten into space by a communist country. The U.S. was going to miss out on the exploration of a great new frontier. They demanded that the government change things.

The government acted on the demand. It formed The National Aeronautics and Space Administration (NASA). From now on, this organization would be in charge of all American space work. The year was 1958. The United States would now enter a race into space with the Soviet Union.

THE FIRST SUCCESSES

While NASA was being formed, the three services went on working separately. The Army scored a success in early 1958 when it launched an unmanned spacecraft called *Explorer 1.* Carried aloft by a Jupiter-C rocket, *Explorer 1* became the first American craft to orbit the earth.

Once NASA got down to work, it put an end to the "race" between the three services. Then it began to launch its own unmanned space shots. The first to go was called *Pioneer 1.* It was aimed at the moon. The craft failed to reach its target, but it did travel more than 80,000 miles into space. A later moon shot—*Pioneer 4*—did better. Launched in March, 1959, it came to within 37,300 miles of the moon.

Though busy with unmanned shots, NASA was even busier with another job. In December, 1958, it started work on a program to send men into space. The program bore a name taken from ancient Greek legend. It was called Project Mercury in honor of the fleet-footed messenger of the Greek gods.

PROJECT MERCURY

Project Mercury wanted to do more than send men into space. It also wanted to bring them home safely. To make sure that the flights would be safe, the project began with a series of unmanned test shots. A spacecraft had been designed for Mercury and the tests were meant to see how well it performed. Like the containers that had carried the Soviet dogs into space, it was called a capsule.

Thirteen test shots took place between September, 1959, and April, 1961. They all sent the capsule riding out into the Atlantic Ocean from the space center that had taken shape at Cape Canaveral, Florida.

In firing the capsule out into the Atlantic, the tests showed a major difference between the American and Soviet space programs. The Russians brought their spacecraft down on land. But the Americans chose to have theirs "splash down" in the water, where they would be picked up by waiting ships. Water landings were thought to be "softer"—and thus far safer—than earth landings.

Of the thirteen shots, six failed because of trouble in the rockets that took the spacecraft aloft. Three others carried animals to see how well living creatures did in space. Launched were two rhesus monkeys—Sam and Miss Sam—and a chimpanzee named Ham. All returned safely and in good health.

When the tests were completed, NASA was ready to try its first manned flights.

THE FIRST SEVEN

While the test shots were being made, NASA searched for the men who would be its first astronauts. Beginning in early 1959, it tested 110 military fliers for the jobs. Seven men were finally chosen. They were all jet pilots.

Three came from the Air Force. They were:

CAPT. LEROY GORDON COOPER
CAPT. VIRGIL "GUS" GRISSOM
CAPT. DONALD "DEKE" SLAYTON

Three were Navy pilots:

LT. MALCOLM SCOTT CARPENTER
LT. COMDR. WALTER "WALLY" SCHIRRA
LT. COMDR. ALAN SHEPARD

One was a Marine Corps flier:

LT. COL. JOHN GLENN

The seven men immediately became national heroes. Their NASA activities made headlines throughout the country. Those activities were many. All were meant to prepare the astronauts for whatever problems space flight might bring. The men went through an intensive physical training program. They rode in whirling centrifuges to accustom them to the heavy pressures of

America's original seven astronauts. Front row, left to right: Walter Schirra, Donald Slayton, John Glenn, Scott Carpenter. Back row, left to right: Alan Shepard, Virgil Grissom, Gordon Cooper.

gravity at lift-off. They floated about in special chambers to prepare them for work when weightless. They were made to endure great heat and high noise levels.

By early 1961, NASA felt ready to try its first manned shots. Planned for the coming months were two flights. Each would carry a single man. Each would be a suborbital journey. This meant that it would carry its astronaut into space but would not place him in orbit. On reaching the edge of space, he would drop back down into the Atlantic.

If both shots went well, NASA would then think it safe to send a man into orbit.

Astronaut Alan Shepard was chosen for the first suborbital flight. He was 37 years old, a slender man who had more than 3,600 hours of flying time in jets. He was married and the father of two girls. The newspapers reported that Shepard loved water skiing and drove a white sports car equipped with racing tires.

DISAPPOINTMENTS

Shepard was told that he would blast off on May 2, 1961. At the time, the Soviets had yet to send Yuri Gagarin skyward. Shepard and his fellow NASA workers knew that the Soviets were working hard on a manned shot. He hoped that he would get up quickly and win the honor of being the first man ever to visit space. But April brought a disappointment. The news of Gagarin's great flight was flashed round the world.

The news brought more than disappointment. It gave NASA a jolting shock. Gagarin had done more than travel to the edge of space as Shepard was going to do. He had gone on to orbit the earth.

Another disappointment came when May 2 dawned. A rainstorm swept in over Cape Canaveral. The control center at the Cape—it was known as Mercury Control—ordered "no go" for the shot two hours before launch time. An impatient Shepard had to wait until May 5 before the weather cleared.

In the early morning darkness that day, the astronaut donned his space suit and rode an elevator up the gantry to his capsule. The capsule, which sat atop an 83-foot-tall Redstone rocket, was shaped like a bell. It measured 9 feet 6 inches long and was 6 feet wide at its base. There was just enough room inside for Shepard to fit into a contour seat.

Stretching upward from the nose of the capsule

was the escape tower. This was a structure consisting of thin steel legs with a small barrel-shaped rocket at their top. The tower was attached to the capsule for safety reasons. Its rocket would fire if anything went wrong with the launch. It would yank Shepard and the capsule free of the Redstone and pull it away to safety. The escape tower, which would be dropped off as the capsule shot into space, was to be a part of every NASA spacecraft.

Shepard had given his capsule a name—*Freedom 7*. The *7* was in honor of the first seven astronauts. All the Project Mercury capsules would have *7* in their names. The astronauts themselves had a private nickname for *Freedom 7*. Because of its round shape, they called it "the garbage can."

THE FLIGHT OF *FREEDOM 7*

Lift-off took place at 9:43 A.M. The Redstone thundered to life and thrust itself upward. Five minutes later, it was approaching an altitude of 116 miles. Along with the escape tower, it broke free of the capsule and fell away. *Freedom 7* was on its own.

The Cape Canaveral area was crowded with people who had come to see Shepard off. They had spent the night in their cars or on the beaches near the space center. Now they held their breaths as the Redstone thundered skyward. Holding their breaths also were millions of television viewers across the country. They all knew that a man might well die before their eyes if anything went wrong. Slowly, they began to breathe easier as the rocket streaked higher and higher. Then they listened to Shepard's calm voice as he checked his instrument panel and reported on the cabin pressure, cabin temperature, and fuel levels. All were normal.

Soon after blasting off, Shepard began to experience the strange feeling of weightlessness. It did not bother him as *Freedom 7* flashed along 116 miles out from the earth. Then it was time for the return. The capsule gave Shepard a bumpy ride when it came hurtling back down through the earth's atmosphere. Suddenly, a giant red-white-and-blue parachute burst from the spacecraft. It slowed the descent. Finally, there was a huge splash as *Freedom 7* ended its journey 302 miles from Cape Canaveral.

Helicopters swept in from a waiting Navy ship, the aircraft carrier *Lake Champlain.* Divers dropped into the sea. They immediately attached large air bags to the capsule to make sure that it stayed

Astronaut Alan Shepard is shown in his Freedom 7 *spacecraft just before it was sealed. His suborbital flight made him the first American in space.*

afloat. Then explosive devices went off automatically and popped the hatch open. Shepard climbed out into the air. A line came down from one of the helicopters and lifted him to safety. Another line was tied to the capsule so that it, too, could be lifted and carried away to the *Lake Champlain.*

Shepard had just one thing to say to the flight crew when he climbed board the helicopter:

"Boy, what a ride!"

The "ride" had lasted 15 minutes and 22 seconds. The United States had sent its first astronaut into space and had brought him safely home.

THE LOSS OF *LIBERTY BELL 7*

NASA tried its second suborbital flight on July 21, 1961. This time, astronaut Virgil "Gus" Grissom was shot out over the Atlantic. He rode in a capsule that he had christened *Liberty Bell 7.* The flight was almost an exact copy of Shepard's "ride." It lasted almost 16 minutes, carried Grissom 118 miles out from the earth, and brought him down in the Atlantic some 300 miles from Cape Canaveral.

By the time of his flight, millions of Americans felt they knew "Gus" Grissom personally. The press had told them all about him. They knew that he had been an Air Force test pilot. They knew that he had flown more than 100 combat missions during the Korean War. And they knew that, at age 35, he was a quiet, modest man. His modesty showed itself whenever he talked of how his capsule would be on automatic pilot throughout the flight. He would say that he was just going along for the ride.

Everything went perfectly for Grissom from lift-off to landing. But then there was trouble. It came after *Liberty Bell 7* struck the water.

As soon as the capsule splashed down, rescue helicopters roared in overhead. Divers plunged into the sea. They began to attach the air bags that would keep *Liberty Bell 7* afloat. But, suddenly, Grissom heard a sound like a gunshot.

He knew right away what had caused it—the explosive devices that were to blow the hatch open. They had gone off ahead of time, before the capsule was floating safely. Water rushed in on the astronaut. He quickly unbuckled his safety harness, scrambled out, and dove over the side. *Liberty Bell 7* began to sink.

A line came speeding down from one of the helicopters. The divers quickly fastened it in place as more and more water poured into the capsule. Grissom's space suit was air-filled and waterproof, and so he stayed in the water and tried to help them. But now he ran into more trouble. His suit was open in one place. It was filling with water.

Grissom was in danger of going under along with his *Liberty Bell.*

Overhead, the helicopter was now struggling to lift the capsule from the waves. But the capsule was so heavy with water that it almost pulled its rescuer into the sea. The helicopter fought back. It was starting to win the battle when a red light flashed on its instrument panel. The light signaled engine trouble. The helicopter had to release the capsule. *Liberty Bell 7* disappeared beneath the surface and was lost forever.

As his spaceship vanished from sight, Grissom was lifted to safety. But even that job caused trouble. He was held prisoner in the water for long moments by the downdraft from the helicopter's whirling rotors.

Later, Grissom's bad luck was rounded out by news from the helicopter crew that had fought so hard to save his capsule. He learned that their red light had flashed in error. Nothing had been wrong with the engine. The third man ever to travel in space had lost his *Liberty Bell 7* for no good reason.

But, despite his loss, the flights that he and Alan Shepard had made to the edge of space had been great successes. NASA was now ready to put a man in orbit.

3.
THE FIRST AMERICAN IN ORBIT

As NASA was preparing to blast its first man into orbit, startling news arrived from the Soviet Union. A second cosmonaut had circled the earth. He was Gherman Titov, the man who had served as the backup pilot for Yuri Gagarin's flight. Titov had lifted off on August 6, 1961, and had stayed aloft for more than 25 hours. He had circled the earth 17 times.

Seventeen orbits! NASA was planning just three orbits for its astronaut. Once again, the Americans had to face the fact that the Russians were still long miles ahead of them in the race to conquer space.

THE TROUBLED ATLAS ROCKET

The news made the NASA workers more impatient than ever to put a man in orbit. But they ran into one problem after another as they attempted to do so. The trouble was caused by the Atlas rocket that was to replace the Redstone used by Shepard and Grissom. The Atlas now had to take over because it was the only U.S. rocket with the power to get a manned capsule up to orbital height. But it was plagued by technical problems that kept it tied to the earth for weeks.

Finally, the Atlas began to work properly. In November, 1961, it placed a capsule in orbit. The capsule circled the earth twice before dropping into the Atlantic. Riding aboard it was a chimpanzee named Enos. His job was to show how well a living creature could work when weightless for two or more hours. The NASA scientists were still worried about what would happen to a weightless man. They had heard that Titov had become sick to his stomach during his long trip.

Enos, however, did a good job. He had been trained to pull a series of levers on command. He obeyed all the commands radioed to him while he was weightless. The NASA scientists felt that not all men would become ill as Titov had.

And so, NASA was now ready for its first manned orbital flight. The astronaut was John Glenn. He christened his capsule *Friendship 7* and got ready to lift off in late December, 1961. But, like Shepard, he had to put up with several delays. His flight was cancelled five times, first because of technical problems and then because of storms over the Atlantic that would have made the lift-off unsafe.

At last, the skies looked clear enough for a launch on February 20, 1962. At 2:30 A.M. that day, Glenn worked his way into his space suit. The sky was black when he arrived at the launch pad, but the Atlas rocket was a blinding white in the glow of the forty-eight searchlights that illuminated it. He rode the elevator up the gantry and settled himself in *Friendship 7.* It was now 6:00 A.M.

FRIENDSHIP 7 LIFTS OFF

John Glenn was 38 years old at the time of his flight. A red-haired man with a freckled face, he was the oldest of the astronauts. He was known as a top fighter pilot who had downed three enemy planes in the final nine days of the Korean War. He had come out of the fighting with twenty-three medals. In 1957, he had set a supersonic speed record in a flight from California to New York. Glenn was married to his childhood sweetheart and was the father of two teenage children.

Cape Canaveral was as crowded this February 20 as it had been for the Shepard and Grissom flights. The space center was filled with U.S. officials and important guests from foreign nations. Thousands of people were gathered on the nearby beaches. Millions more across the nation and the world were seated tensely in front of their television sets and radios. All were waiting for the moment when there would be a thunderous roar and the white arrowlike Atlas would charge upward through clouds of smoke.

That moment came at 9:47 A.M. The countdown ended in Mercury Control. There was ignition. Flames burst from the base of the Atlas. The rocket stood dead still for several seconds. Then, when its engines had built up enough power to lift it free of the pad, it moved into the air. Seconds later, the Atlas was flashing deep into the morning sky.

Glenn radioed Mercury Control that he was having a bumpy ride as he gathered more and more speed. Next, on reaching orbital height, he said the Atlas had successfully broken away from

John Glenn, the first American to orbit the earth, readies himself for launch in Friendship 7. *He circled the earth three times.*

Friendship 7. Then, as the capsule began to travel through orbit, he reported that he was weightless but feeling fine.

STRANGE AND WONDERFUL SIGHTS

As Shepard and Grissom had done before him, Glenn talked of the wonderful view that was to be had from space. Out of one window, he could see a giant cloud formation over Cape Canaveral. Out the other, he could see the Canary Islands off the coast of Africa. Glenn had one word for the scene: magnificent.

Friendship 7 shot eastward across the Atlantic and headed for the distant Pacific Ocean. Glenn was treated to another wonderful sight when his path took him over Australia. It was still dark there, and the people of the city of Perth left their lights on to serve as a beacon for him. When he looked down, he could see a vast glow. It was made up of more than half a million electric lights.

Then a mysterious sight greeted the astronaut. Glenn was above the Pacific and the sun was just coming up. He radioed that he could see thousands of tiny lights just outside his window. He said they were yellowish-green and glowed like tiny fireflies. He did not know what they were.

The scientists at Mercury Control thought he was "seeing things." They changed their minds when astronauts on later flights noticed the same lights. In the end, Glenn's "fireflies" turned out to be water droplets from the cooling radiator on his spacecraft. When they shot out of the radiator, the droplets froze and became crystals that glowed in the sunlight.

TROUBLE IN ORBIT

Trouble showed itself as Glenn ended his first orbit. He reported that *Friendship 7* was tending to drift to the right as it moved along on automatic pilot. There were small jet engines—called thrusters—attached to the sides of the spacecraft. They were fired automatically from time to time and were meant to keep the capsule on a straight course. But there was a technical problem in one. It was causing the drift.

Glenn tried to solve things by cutting off the automatic pilot. He took over the controls and guided the rest of the mission himself. The trouble did not end, however. The capsule took on a spinning action as it whipped through space.

At one point, Mercury Control asked Glenn if

he wanted to end his spinning flight early or go for the scheduled three orbits. The astronaut replied that he was ready for the three orbits.

More trouble then cropped up. One of the instrument panels in Mercury Control suddenly showed a red light. It warned of trouble with the plexiglass shield that covered *Friendship 7.* The shield was to protect the capsule during the trip down from orbit. As usual, friction would cause a searing heat when the capsule hit the earth's atmosphere. The shield would then burn away. In doing so, it would absorb much of the heat and safeguard *Friendship 7* and its astronaut from being burned to ash.

But now the red light was flashing. What exactly did it mean? Was the light misbehaving? Or was it warning that the shield was coming loose and might fly off at any moment? If it tore itself away, Glenn and his ship would both die within seconds of entering the earth's atmosphere.

One question was bigger than all the rest. What could be done to help keep the shield in place if indeed it was coming loose? The scientists discussed the matter for long minutes. At last, they decided on an answer.

Strapped to *Friendship 7* was a "retropack." This was a container holding the three retro-rockets that were the ship's "brakes." On being fired near journey's end, they would slow the capsule so that it could begin its descent to the Atlantic. Once they had done their job, the flip of a switch would free their package from the spaceship and send it floating away. The scientists decided to leave the package strapped to *Friendship 7.* Perhaps it would hold the shield in place long enough for it to do its job of absorbing the deadly heat.

SOME WILD MINUTES

Near the end of his third orbit, Glenn was again above the Pacific. The time was at hand for his return to earth. The retro-rockets were fired, with the package then being allowed to remain in place. *Friendship 7* started its descent. And Glenn entered a period of 23 wild minutes.

The spacecraft struck the earth's atmosphere. It began to jolt from side to side. Glenn saw a fiery glow outside his window. Then chunks of flaming red went hurtling past. Did they come from the heat shield? Was the shield coming off? Or were they burning chunks from the retropack? Glenn had no idea. His problems were topped off by his radio. It blacked out. The blackout was caused by heavy gases that took shape around the spaceship because of the heat.

For long moments, the people in Mercury Control did not know whether the astronaut was alive or burned to a cinder. Then his radio came back to life. They sighed with relief when they heard his first words:

"Boy, that was a real fireball."

Friendship 7 was bucking wildly from side to side as Glenn spoke. Worse, the Atlantic was coming into view and the capsule was plummeting nose-first toward the water. Glenn reached for the switch that would release the smaller of the spaceship's two parachutes. It was called the drogue chute. Its job was to brake and steady the capsule before the main parachute was released. Glenn hoped it would steady the ship enough to avoid a head-on crash into the sea. But, just before he touched the switch, both the drogue and the main chute were automatically triggered. Out they rushed to snap open with a thunderclap above *Friendship 7.* The spaceship abruptly slowed and righted itself.

The 23-minute wild ride was over. Glenn floated down to the Atlantic. He splashed into the water at 2:43 P.M. The destroyer *Noa* was six miles away and standing by to pick him up. It opened its engines wide and sped to *Friendship 7.*

Despite the problems with the spacecraft, John Glenn's flight was called a great success. The astronaut had circled the earth three times. From lift-off to splashdown, his journey had lasted 4 hours and 55 minutes. In that time, Glenn had traveled 83,540 miles. He had overcome one danger after another. He had been weightless for hours and had worked well all the while.

NASA was ready for its next strides forward in the race into space.

4.

THE FIRST SPACE WALKS

The Soviet Union and the United States did much fine space work in the years following John Glenn's flight. But, no matter how hard the U.S. tried to catch up, the Soviets went on holding their long lead.

NEW SOVIET FIRSTS

The Russians launched the world's first "group space flight" in August, 1962. This means that they had two ships in orbit at the same time. Cosmonaut Andrian Nikolayev blasted off in a spaceship known as *Vostok 3.* One day later, cosmonaut Papel Popovich shot into orbit aboard *Vostok 4.* The two circled the earth for several days. They did not fly together, but they did come within 3.1 miles from each other during one orbit.

A second Russian "group flight" took off in June, 1963, when Valery Bykovsky rode *Vostok 5* into orbit. Two days later, *Vostok 6* came up. Again, the two ships did not travel together. At one point, however, *Vostok 6* was within three miles of Bykovsky. Bykovsky posted a record journey of 81 orbits.

But it was *Vostok 6* that captured all the headlines. Riding in the spacecraft was a woman cosmonaut—26-year-old Valentina Tereshkova. To her went the honor of being the first woman ever to travel in space. Tereshkova circled the earth 48 times.

NEW MERCURY FLIGHTS

And what was the United States doing during this time? Between May, 1962, and May, 1963, NASA placed three astronauts in space. Malcolm Scott Carpenter went first and rode *Aurora 7* through three orbits. Walter "Wally" Schirra was the next to lift off. His *Sigma 7* completed six orbits before splashing down in the Pacific Ocean. Schirra was the first astronaut to land in the Pacific.

The third flight was the longest attempted by Project Mercury. Leroy Gordon Cooper flew the mission in *Faith 7.* He circled the earth 22 times.

The trip went well, but ran into trouble at its end. An electrical problem killed the automatic pilot. As *Faith 7* was bucking its way down through the earth's atmosphere, Cooper had to take the controls and guide the spacecraft to a safe landing.

By now, six of the original seven astronauts had been in space. The only one of their number not to go up was Donald "Deke" Slayton. He was "grounded" when he developed a heart problem. The problem was a minor one, but NASA wanted to take no chances with his life by sending him aloft. Slayton went on to do excellent work on the ground for NASA.

Gordon Cooper's flight was not only the longest tried in the Mercury program. It was also the last one launched by the project. NASA now turned to two new programs. Both were far more ambitious than Mercury had been. They were called the Gemini and Apollo programs. They would start with Gemini.

GEMINI AND APOLLO

The Gemini program was named for a formation of stars. The people of ancient times thought that the formation looked like two men sitting together. The name was chosen because the program would be using capsules able to carry two men.

NASA planned to send the capsules into space atop the newly developed Titan rocket. The Titan was far more powerful than the Atlas used in Project Mercury. The Titan had 530,000 pounds of thrusting power. That was 104,000 more pounds of thrust than the Atlas could provide.

Gemini was to send out twelve flights aboard the giant Titan. Each was meant to help pave the way toward the Apollo program.

The Apollo program was named for the Greek god of sunlight, poetry, and music. The program would see NASA's people take on the greatest work they had ever attempted. Its aim was to do what had never been done before—place a man on the moon.

The moon! Hanging out there in space a quarter of a million miles away, it had always been far beyond man's reach. But all the NASA workers were determined to send a man there. Their determination came from President John F. Kennedy.

Back in 1961, just three weeks after Alan Shepard's suborbital flight, Mr. Kennedy had delivered a speech to Congress. In it, he had expressed his worry that the Soviets were still leading in the conquest of space. He then went on to set a goal for the United States. He said the nation would make an all-out effort to place a man on the moon by the end of the 1960s.

Gemini started the country on the road to that goal. The final steps would be taken by the Apollo program.

GEMINI BEGINS

The Gemini program began with two unmanned flights, *Gemini 1* and *2.* Both were tests of the new two-man capsules. The first shot took place in 1964. The second followed in early 1965. Both proved successful. Beginning with the next launch—*Gemini 3*—all the flights carried astronauts.

By the time Gemini began its launches in 1964, the United States had been visited by a tragedy. President Kennedy had died of an assassin's bullets. Cape Canaveral had been renamed in his honor, and the space center there had become the Kennedy Space Center. The Cape was later given back it original name, but the space center went on bearing the young president's name.

And, by the time of the launches, NASA had

increased the number of its astronauts. Twenty-three new men had been welcomed to space work. Thirteen of these rookies would make the Gemini manned flights. Of the thirteen, five were Navy officers:

EUGENE CERNAN

CHARLES "PETE" CONRAD

RICHARD GORDON

JAMES LOVELL

JOHN YOUNG

Seven were Air Force pilots:

EDWIN "BUZZ" ALDRIN

FRANK BORMAN

MICHAEL COLLINS

JAMES McDIVITT

DAVID SCOTT

THOMAS STAFFORD

EDWARD WHITE

And one was a civilian—an aeronautical engineer:

NEIL ARMSTRONG

GEMINI 3: A TEST

Gemini 3 gave the two-man capsule its first test with astronauts aboard. The mission took NASA veteran "Gus" Grissom and newcomer John Young into orbit on March 25, 1965. They made three circles of the earth before splashing down. Grissom set a personal record on the trip. He became the first astronaut to visit space twice.

GEMINI 4: A WALK IN SPACE

With a moon shot looming in the future, NASA wanted to see how its men did on long-distance flights. NASA also wanted the astronauts to leave the ships for space walks. The technical term for a space walk is "extra-vehicular activity (EVA)." The walks would help train the astronauts to make the outside repairs that might be needed on a long journey. In addition, the walks would show whether the men would be able to move about easily in their heavy space suits when working on the moon.

James McDivitt and Edward White tried their hands at both jobs in Gemini 4. They left the earth on June 3, 1965. By the time they returned four days later, they had completed 62 orbits. Theirs was NASA's longest flight to date.

The high point of the trip came on its first day. As their capsule orbited the earth for the third time, Edward White checked his space suit and helmet. At his side, James McDivitt lowered the pressure in the cabin so that it matched that outside. Then McDivitt opened the hatch above White's head. White stood up and stepped out into space.

White held a small gunlike device in his gloved hand. Whenever he squeezed its trigger, it gave off spurts of nitrogen. They enabled him to move around the spaceship. He remained connected to it by means of a long nylon cord that was attached to his waist. The cord was known as a tether.

On leaving the capsule, White stared at the vast scene around him. There was blackness stretching away deep into space. But, all at the same time, he could see the sun, the moon, and many distant stars.

In airless space, he had the feeling that he and the capsule were not moving. But such was not the case at all. The two of them were hurtling along at 17,500 miles an hour.

The hand-held device ran out of nitrogen in about three minutes. White now moved around the spacecraft by pulling on his tether. He floated from one side of the ship to the other and then hovered above it. Because the capsule was weightless, he found that he could turn it in dif-

*Edward White, the first American to "walk" in space. Secured to the
Gemini 4 spacecraft by a tether, he moved about by means of the
gunlike device held in his right hand.*

ferent directions with each pull of the tether. The
astronaut weighed 170 pounds. But he was able
to tug the 7,500-pound capsule about as if it were
a toy on a string.

White was scheduled to "walk" in space for 20

minutes. When the time was up, he wanted to remain outside. He told McDivitt that they had more than three days in space ahead of them. It wouldn't hurt to walk a while longer. He was having too good a time to come back in. But Gemini Control insisted that he return to his seat. With a sigh, the astronaut floated down through the open hatchway.

Edward White had spent 21 minutes outside the capsule and had become the first American to walk in space.

White, however, was not *the* first man to walk in space. Again, the Russians had beaten the Americans to the punch. On March 8, 1965— three months before *Gemini 4* lifted off—cosmonaut Alexei Leonov had won the honor of being the world's first space walker. He had spent 10 minutes outside his craft.

GEMINI 5: THE LONGEST MISSION

Gemini 5 lifted off on August 21, 1965. The mission had a single goal—to see how men would fare on an extremely long journey. *Gemini 5* was to remain in orbit for eight days—the length of time it would take a spacecraft to reach the moon and then return home. Gordon Cooper and

Charles Conrad rode the capsule into space and then spent the entire flight struggling with one technical problem after another. Time and again, Gemini Control thought it would have to bring them down ahead of schedule. But they held on for the eight days and landed after 120 orbits.

Everyone at NASA was jubilant. *Gemini 5* had set a magnificent record. It was the longest space flight to that time. It had far surpassed cosmonaut Valery Bykovsky's 1963 flight in *Vostok 5*. *Vostok 5* had completed 81 orbits. Cooper and Conrad had bested that total by 39 orbits.

NASA said that *Gemini 5*'s accomplishment had at last sent the United States forging ahead of the Soviet Union. But better things were yet to come. They began with *Gemini 6* and *7*.

GEMINI 6 AND *7*: A MEETING IN SPACE

Gemini 6 and *7* traveled in space together. Their assignment was to practice the tricky job of inching their capsules up to each other. The Soviets had launched two "group flights" in 1961. The Russian ships had not flown together but had come to about three miles from each other. *Gemini 6* and *7* were to draw much closer. They were to end up inches apart.

The mission was a rehearsal for a job that would need to be done on a moon flight. The spaceship that flew to the moon would have to "dock" with another at one point in its journey. This meant that it would have to lock onto the other so that the two of them could travel as if they were one.

Gemini 6 and *7* were on their way in mid-December, 1965. In *Gemini 6* were Wally Schirra and Thomas Stafford, while Frank Borman and James Lovell piloted *Gemini 7*. When the ships swung into orbit, they were about 1,200 miles apart. Immediately, they headed toward each other. Five hours later, a mere 40 yards lay between them.

The capsules were now so close that their crews could see each other. In *Gemini 7*, Lovell looked out at Schirra across the way and radioed that he could see him moving his lips. Schirra radioed back that he was chewing gum.

Gemini 7's job was now to hold a steady course. In *Gemini 6*, Schirra and Stafford inched over until they were about a foot away from *7*. The two ships flew side by side for a few seconds. Then Schirra and Stafford moved off. But they returned again—and again—and again—until they had proved that spaceships can fly safely with a scant few feet between them. Then the two capsules

Gemini 6 and Gemini 7 practice docking maneuvers. The two spacecraft came to within inches of each other.

separated to a distance of about 100 feet. They held that distance as they whipped along for the next 20 hours.

GEMINI 8: THE FIRST SPACE DOCKING

Once *Gemini 6* and *7* had done their job, Neil Armstrong and David Scott took the next step. They set out to make the first docking ever tried

in space. Their mission began when a rocket—
called an Agena—was fired into orbit in March,
1966. About two hours later, Armstrong and Scott
went chasing after it in *Gemini 8.*

On swinging into orbit, the two astronauts
spent some six hours closing in on the rocket.
Their capsule and the Agena were both equipped
with special devices that would lock the two
vehicles together when they touched. Carefully,
Armstrong and Scott moved in on the Agena.
There was a slight bump. Switches were flipped.
The two ships were locked together.

NASA had another triumph to its credit. *Gemini
8* had made the world's first space docking.

But then things went wrong—very wrong. *Gemini 8* tried to move forward with the Agena. The
two vehicles suddenly began to tumble wildly
through space. Desperately, the astronauts tried
various moves to end the tumbling. But nothing
worked. They had to break contact with the
Agena. Armstrong and Stafford returned safely to
earth. The Agena sailed on in orbit. It would play
a part in a later Gemini mission.

GEMINI 9-12: DOCKINGS AND SPACE WALKS

The rest of the Gemini flights took place between June and November, 1966. They all prac-

ticed docking in space. In *Gemini 9,* Eugene Cernan and Tom Stafford quickly closed in on the Agena rocket that had been fired into orbit ahead of them. But they met with failure when they tried to dock. The equipment in the Agena was at fault. It was jammed.

Gemini 10 made a successful docking with its Agena rocket in July. Then it moved the rocket through space without the tumbling problem that had bothered *Gemini 8.* Flying the *Gemini 10* mission were Michael Collins and John Young.

Another successful docking was posted in September, this one by Charles Conrad and Richard Gordon in *Gemini 11.* In fact, they made two successful dockings. After completing the first, they broke away from their Agena, moved off, and then returned for a second docking.

A final docking was made during the *Gemini 12* mission, which was flown by Edwin "Buzz" Aldrin and James Lovell. The flight was the last in the Gemini program.

The *Gemini 9–12* flights also featured a series of space walks. The walks saw the astronauts practice a number of different jobs. Eugene Cernan started things off by spending two hours outside the *Gemini 9* capsule. Michael Collins followed with two walks during *Gemini 10.*

On the first, he hovered in the spaceship's open hatchway and took photographs of the surroundings. Just before his second walk, *Gemini 10* came up alongside the Agena that had been left behind by the *Gemini 8* crew. Floating at the end of a long tether, Collins made his way over to the Agena and removed a package of scientific gear that was attached to it. Collins spent about 40 minutes on the walk.

Gemini 11 sent Richard Gordon on two walks. They kept him outside for 2 hours and 47 minutes.

A space walk record was set by "Buzz" Aldrin on *Gemini 12.* He made three walks and performed tasks while dangling at the end of his tether. On one walk, he installed a handrail on the Agena rocket. On another, he worked with a special wrench that had been designed for use in space. Altogether, Aldrin spent 5 hours and 37 minutes away from his ship.

And so Gemini's work was done. The flights had shown that NASA was ready to take the next step in making President Kennedy's dream come true—the dream of placing a man on the moon by the end of the 1960s. The time had come for the Apollo program.

5.

THE FIRST
MEN TO
THE MOON

The beginning work on the Apollo program was carried out while the Gemini missions were being flown. That work saw the development of the Apollo space vehicles to go to the moon and the rocket to get them there.

THE APOLLO EQUIPMENT

The new rocket was called Saturn 5. It was to do two jobs. First, it was to fire a moon flight up into orbit around the earth. Then it was to blast the flight out of orbit and send it on its way to the moon.

So that it could do these jobs, the rocket was

divided into three sections, called stages. The first stage would lift the astronauts away from Cape Kennedy. It would be released and left to float away when it had used up its fuel. Next, the second stage would send them up to earth orbit. Then it, too, would be released. The third stage would provide needed extra speed while in orbit. Then it would fire them off toward the moon.

Saturn 5 was a giant. It stood some 280 feet tall on its launching pad and made the Mercury and Gemini rockets look like midgets. It had a thrusting power of over 9 million pounds. The rocket needed all the power it could muster because it had to carry 5.6 million pounds of fuel and lift all three of the modules of the new Apollo spacecraft.

THE COMMAND MODULE

The three parts of the Apollo spaceship were known as modules because they were built to fit together. The first was the Command Module (CM). This was the capsule in which the astronauts would ride. Sitting perched atop the Saturn, the CM was shaped like a cone and was built to carry three men. It measured almost 12 feet wide and about 11 feet long.

THE SERVICE MODULE

Next in line was the large, barrel-shaped Service Module (SM). It was connected to the base of the Command Module so that the two could fly together as one. The Service Module got its name from the equipment stored inside it—equipment that would provide oxygen and power. The power would come from a rocket engine at the base of the SM.

The Command Module and the Service Module would be attached to each other throughout the journey. On arrival at the moon, the rocket engine on the SM would brake the vehicle so that it would go into lunar orbit. Later, when the moon journey was over, the engine would be used to start the spacecraft on its return to the earth. Only when it returned to the earth's atmosphere would the SM be cut away so that there would be as little weight as possible at splashdown.

Because the two modules would spend so much time linked together, the NASA scientists thought of them as a single unit and called them the Command/Service Module (CSM). When the CSM was set in place atop the Saturn rocket, the whole rig stood more than 300 feet tall.

THE LUNAR MODULE

The third module was the Lunar Module (LM). Looking something like a spider because it was equipped with four spindly legs, this was the vehicle that would actually land on the moon.

At the start of the moon flight, the LM would ride inside the Saturn's third stage. Once that third stage had blasted the astronauts out of earth orbit and toward the moon, they would set the LM free. They would then turn their Command/Service Module about, move to the LM, dock with it, and lock in on the Lunar Module. Then, with the LM firmly attached, the engine in the Service Module would be fired. Off the Command/Service Module and the Lunar Module would go toward the moon.

Once in lunar orbit, two of the three astronauts would crawl through a hatchway from the Command Module and enter the Lunar Module. They would break it free and go down to the lunar surface while their companion piloted the CSM far above and awaited their return. At the end of their visit to the moon, they would lift off in the LM and return to the CSM for the trip home.

These necessary dockings—on the trip out from

earth and at the start of the return from the moon—were the reasons for the practice dockings in the Gemini program.

To get the astronauts to and from the lunar surface, the Lunar Module was made up of two sections—the Descent and Ascent Stages. Each contained a rocket engine. The engine in the Descent Stage would provide the power to get the LM down to the moon and bring it in for a landing on its spindly legs. The Ascent Stage engine would carry the Lunar Module back to the Command/Service Module at the end of the visit.

The Lunar Module was an engineering marvel. Any spaceship that landed on the moon needed a launching pad to get back off again. The LM came equipped with its own pad. At the end of a moon visit, the astronauts would fire the Ascent Stage engine. The Ascent Stage would break free and speed away from the lunar surface. Left behind would be the Descent Stage, along with the LM's legs.

THE FIRST APOLLO LAUNCHES

As did Gemini, Apollo began with unmanned test flights. Three tests were made in 1966. They lifted off from Launch Pad 39-A at Cape Kennedy.

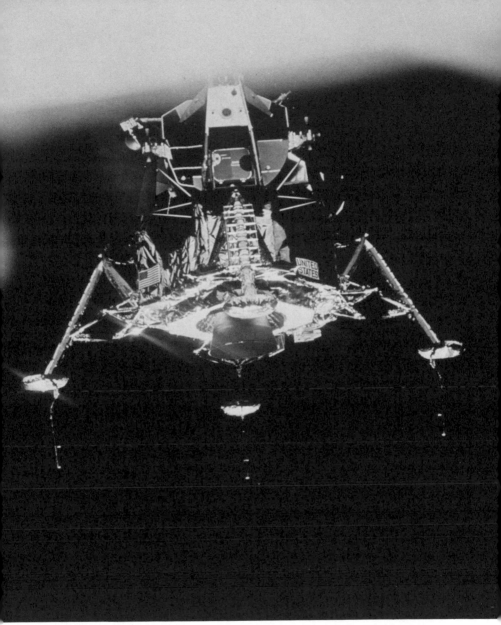

The Lunar Module. The circular device at the base of the LM is the Descent Engine.

The Ascent Stage of the Lunar Module approaches the CSM during rendezvous above the moon. This photograph, taken from the CSM, shows the moon's Sea of Fertility.

It was to serve as the launch pad for every Apollo flight. All the flights would be controlled from a center that had been built at Houston, Texas. Called the NASA Manned Space Flight Center, it became known the world over as Mission Control.

The manned Apollo flights were to be handled mostly by the astronauts who had joined NASA just before the Gemini program. Also taking part would be newcomers who had been selected in 1965 and 1966. The first manned launch, however, was assigned to one of the seven original astronauts—"Gus" Grissom. His companions were to be Roger Chaffee and Gemini veteran Edward White. White was the astronaut who had been the first American to walk in space.

Their flight was planned for February, 1967. It never took place. Tragedy struck the three a few weeks before the launch.

"FIRE IN THE SPACECRAFT"

Early in the afternoon of January 27, 1967, the three astronauts climbed into their capsule atop the giant Saturn rocket on Pad 39-A. Dressed in their space suits, they looked as if they were about to lift off for the moon. But such was not

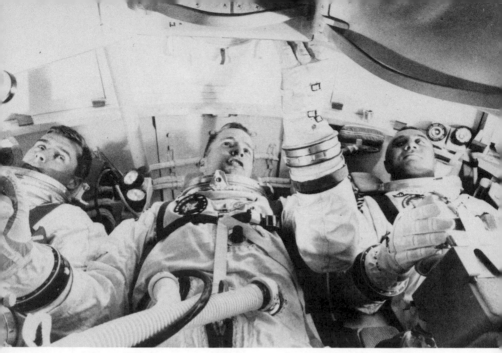

Practicing for what was planned as the first manned Apollo flight are, left to right, Edward White, Roger Chaffee, and Virgil Grissom. The three astronauts died when fire broke out in their spacecraft.

to be the case. Instead, they were to practice the work that would be done when Mission Control counted down through the hours, minutes, and seconds to the actual launch.

The practice countdown lasted the whole afternoon and went on into the early evening. The clock in Mission Control showed 6:31 P.M. when seven terrifying words burst from the capsule's radio. They sent a chill through the listeners.

"We've got a fire in the spacecraft!"

Flames had broken out in the ship's electrical system. In the next instant, they swept through the capsule. They moved with lightning speed because the air in the capsule was 100 percent oxygen as part of the practice session. Cries of pain came through the radio. Chaffee shouted, "We've got a bad fire. Let's get out. We're burning up!" They were the last words heard from the trapped astronauts. The heat caused the capsule's skin to split open. Smoke poured out into the evening air. By then, the three astronauts were dead.

The tragedy plunged the United States into mourning. And it wounded the Apollo program deeply. Further work on the moon launches was put off while engineers investigated the burned capsule and made safety improvements in its design. The program stopped and did not start again until a year later.

The United States was not alone in its loss. Just three months after the Apollo fire, the Soviets sent cosmonaut Vladimir Komarov into orbit aboard a new spacecraft. The ship performed beautifully, only to have its parachutes fail to open as it was landing. Komarov was killed when the craft smashed into the ground.

Then, in 1968, the Soviet Union lost its greatest space hero. Yuri Gagarin died in a plane crash.

A NEW BEGINNING

The Apollo program began again in early 1968 with two unmanned flights. The first, *Apollo 5,* sent the Lunar Module into earth orbit for a test. The second, *Apollo 6,* put the improved capsule to a test.

Apollo 7 became the program's first manned flight. Wally Schirra, Walter Cunningham, and Donn Eisele took the Command/Service Module up into earth orbit and gave it a complete check. They departed on October 11, 1968, and splashed down on October 22 after completing 163 orbits.

Now it was time for the most ambitious Apollo launch to date. *Apollo 8* blasted off on Sunday, December 21, 1968, and set out to establish a magnificent space first for the United States. It was going to carry its three astronauts—Frank Borman, James Lovell, and William Anders—almost a quarter of a million miles away from the earth. If things went well, they would become the first men to reach the moon.

The three would not land on the moon, however. Rather, they would fly in orbit around it. Their job was to see how the Apollo equipment performed on an actual moon flight and to check the lunar surface for good spots for a future landing.

As usual, thousands of people came to Cape Kennedy and gathered along the beaches near the space center to see the launch. They and the countless people who watched on television were treated to a perfect lift-off. The Saturn's first stage sent the CSM up through a sunny sky to a height of more than 120 miles. The second stage put the astronauts into earth orbit. The third stage flicked them out of orbit and started them toward the moon. Since they were not going to land on the moon, they did not take the LM with them.

IN DEEP SPACE

As they streaked into deep space, the three men looked down and saw the earth as no one had ever seen it before. They were now so high that they saw the world as a complete globe. Frank Borman radioed Mission Control that the people at the southern tip of South America should get out their raincoats. He could see storm clouds heading their way.

Though the CSM was operating beautifully, the astronauts began to have some difficulty. They radioed that they seemed to be coming down with some sort of flu. Borman reported having chills and a headache. He became so ill for a time that he vomited.

The illness, which passed after a while, did not keep the three men from going about their work. They kept a constant check on the CSM and sent down their first television pictures of the earth to Mission Control. The pictures were then relayed to television sets across the world. The pictures did not turn out well. In them, the earth appeared as a white blob. Pictures taken the next day were much better and gave television viewers everywhere a clear view of their planet.

On the second day out, the astronauts recorded a space first. They became the first men to leave the pull of the earth's gravity. The gravitational pull of the moon now took over.

That same day saw more pictures travel down to the world's television sets. The pictures were breathtaking. They showed the earth as a colorful disc in space. The waters of the oceans were a deep blue. Cloud formations were a brilliant white. The color brown marked the land areas. Borman told the viewers that they were seeing themselves from 180,000 miles out in space.

CHRISTMAS EVE IN SPACE

The flight entered its fourth day on December 24. On earth, it was Christmas Eve. A quarter of a million miles out in space, it was the day when the Command/Service Module reached its destination. On arrival, it went whirling around to the back side of the moon and gave the United States another space first. The three astronauts became the first men ever to get a first-hand view of the moon's far side. They took photographs of its gray, desolate surface as they streaked along.

While behind the moon, the astronauts were cut off from radio contact with the earth. For long minutes, Mission Control waited for word of how they were faring. Then, suddenly, the CSM swept around to the moon's front side. The radio crackled to life. The astronauts reported that, as had been planned, they had fired the rocket engine in the CSM. The firing had been successful and had put the CSM into lunar orbit. They were now circling the moon at an altitude of about 60 miles.

As the CSM moved through orbit, the astronauts studied the surface below. They looked for and marked their lunar maps with areas that could serve as possible sites for a future landing. They continued to send down television pictures of the surface. Along with the pictures went voice descriptions of what was being seen.

Borman told Mission Control that the surface

looked like "a vast, lonely, forbidding place, an expanse of nothing." He added that it did not look like "a very good place to live and work."

Anders said that the surface had been bombarded through the ages by countless meteorites. He could see the holes and craters they had made on hitting the surface. They looked like pockmarks. They were everywhere.

Lovell reported on one of the moon's most famous landmarks—the Sea of Tranquility. He said it looked like an expanse of dirty, grayish beach.

Late Christmas Eve, Borman said that he was to have delivered a Christmas prayer at his church that night. He added that he just couldn't get to the church. And so he offered up a prayer for worldwide peace as he circled the moon. Borman asked Mission Control to send a tape recording of the prayer to his church. He said the prayer was meant not only for his church but for the whole world.

A little later, the three men read passages from the Bible for the listening world. As they spoke, their television camera took pictures of the desolate lunar surface. At the end of their readings, the astronauts wished the world a Merry Christmas from space.

SIX LONG MINUTES

On Christmas morning, the preparations for the return to earth began. The astronauts gave the Command/Service Module a thorough check and found that everything was continuing to work perfectly.

Then, as they once again moved around to the back side of the moon, they fired the rocket engine in the CSM. It took them out of lunar orbit so that they could head for home.

All was going well in the spacecraft. But there was tension down in Mission Control. As expected, radio contact had been lost when the CSM went behind the moon. But, as was *not* expected, the spacecraft did not come back from behind the moon at the scheduled time. The workers in Mission Control stared at each other. Had something gone wrong? They asked themselves that question for six long minutes after the CSM should have reappeared. Then a sigh of relief went through the room. Lovell's voice was heard. All was well.

Apollo 8—carrying the first men ever to reach the moon and circle it—was heading home after orbiting its target 10 times in 20 hours.

GETTING READY FOR A MOON LANDING

Apollo 8 was a magnificent accomplishment that helped pave the way to the greatest accomplishment of all—an actual moon landing. But more work was needed before NASA dared to try the landing.

That work was done between March and May, 1969. Astronauts tested the Lunar Module with men aboard. First, James McDivitt, David Scott, and Russell Schweickart went into earth orbit in *Apollo 9.* While circling the globe, they docked with the Saturn's third stage, released the Lunar Module, and locked in on it. It was the first time the two modules had linked up and flown together.

Next, McDivitt and Schweickart crawled through a hatchway in the nose of the Command Module and entered the LM. Then they broke away and maneuvered the LM on its own. They traveled 113 miles out from the CSM and returned for a docking. This was another first for NASA—the first time the Lunar Module had flown by itself.

Apollo 10 served as a final test before the moon landing. Carrying Thomas Stafford, John Young, and Eugene Cernan, it sent the CSM and the LM to the moon. Once in lunar orbit, Stafford and Cernan flew the LM for eight hours. During their flight, they came to 9.7 miles from the lunar surface.

And now it was time for the greatest Apollo flight of all—and the greatest journey ever attempted by man. The Apollo launches had started just six years ago. Now *Apollo 11* was ready to try for a moon landing.

6.

THE FIRST MEN ON THE MOON

The voice at Mission Control counted off the final seconds:

"Eight . . . seven . . . six . . . five . . . four . . ."

The giant Saturn rocket stood poised on Pad 39-A at Cape Kennedy. Its white body glistened in the sunlight on this Wednesday, July 16, 1969.

"Three . . . two . . . one. We have ignition . . ."

The time was exactly 9:32 in the morning. Orange flames exploded with a roar at the base of the rocket. Black smoke poured across the pad. For nine seconds, the Saturn did not move as its engines built up enough power to lift it into the air. Then the four steel arms that held it in place fell away. The rocket thrust itself upward.

At first, it rose slowly. But it steadily gathered speed. Twelve seconds after ignition, the Saturn was streaking through the sky. Its guidance system tilted the rocket's nose slightly. The tilt sent the ship flashing out over the Atlantic Ocean.

More than a million people were gathered in the Cape Kennedy area to see the lift-off. The space center itself was crowded with officials from the U.S. government and from foreign nations. On hand were more than 3,400 news reporters from fifty-six countries. President Richard Nixon watched on a television set in his White House office. Watching with him were 500 million television viewers across the world. Millions more listened in on their radios. They all held their breath as the *Apollo 11* mission headed into space. If all went well, two of the astronauts in the Command/Service Module would walk on the moon just a few days from now.

RIDERS TO THE MOON

There were three astronauts in the CSM. They were Neil Armstrong, Edwin "Buzz" Aldrin, and Michael Collins. All three were space veterans.

They had been among the men who had become astronauts at the start of the Gemini program.

Neil Armstrong had made the world's first docking in space on the *Gemini 8* mission. Unlike most of the astronauts who had been on hand for Gemini, he was not a military man. Rather, he was a civilian—an aeronautical engineer. Armstrong was the commander of the *Apollo 11* mission. He was scheduled to be the first man ever to walk on the moon.

"Buzz" Aldrin would be the second man on the moon. He had come to NASA from the Air Force. On *Gemini 12,* he had set a record for space walks when he ventured outside his capsule three times for a total of five and a half hours. It was a record that no one had yet broken.

Michael Collins had also come to NASA from the Air Force. He had made two space walks while out with *Gemini 9.* His job on *Apollo 11* was to fly the CSM in orbit while Armstrong and Aldrin rode the Lunar Module down to the moon. Collins was well known for his sense of humor. He often joked that he would be the "forgotten man" on the flight. He said that no one would ever forget what Armstrong and Aldrin did. But he would be remembered only as "old what's-his-name."

Checking out **Apollo 11**'s *Command Module before heading for the moon are, left to right: Neil Armstrong, commander; Michael Collins, Command Module pilot; Edwin Aldrin, Lunar Module pilot*

"IT'S REALLY MOVING, BABE."

The Apollo spaceship in which the three men rode was named *Columbia*. As it was thrust skyward, they checked its instrument panel and radioed Mission Control that all was well. Their voices were calm and businesslike. Only once did they show how excited they really were. One voice said, "Wow, what a ride! It's really moving, babe."

The Saturn's first stage burned for a little over two minutes. By now, the rocket was a mere speck in the sky. When the stage burned itself out, it was sent floating off into space. The second stage was fired. It placed the CSM into earth orbit. Then, as soon as the stage completed its work, it was cut free.

For the next two and a half hours, the men in *Columbia* readied themselves for the firing of the third stage. When it was ignited, it shot the CSM out of orbit and hurled it toward the moon. *Columbia* now broke away from the third stage. The astronauts turned the CSM around. They guided it to the upper end of the third stage where the Lunar Module, *Eagle,* was stored.

There was a slight bump as *Columbia's* nose came against the LM. A flick of a switch locked the two ships together. The CSM backed off and pulled the little craft free. Then, with *Eagle* firmly attached, the CSM headed for the moon. The third stage whirled away into space.

The world watched and listened as *Columbia* sped deeper and deeper into space. Neil Armstrong looked out the window at his side and told Mission Control that he could see all of the North American continent. The view stretched down to South America. Then, he said, he ran out of window.

A short time later, the astronauts brought out their color television cameras. Down to Mission Control went pictures of the earth's surface. Seen mainly was the Pacific Ocean. This caused "Buzz" Aldrin to grin and ask if Mission Control could tilt the earth so that he could pick up some shots of land. Mission Control joked back: "I don't think we can do that." The pictures were put on tape at Mission Control. They were later shown to the entire world.

DAYS OF ADVENTURE

The remainder of *Apollo 11*'s first day in space went smoothly. (The same held true for the second and third days.) Armstrong, Aldrin, and Collins checked *Columbia*'s instruments, rested, exercised, and sent back television pictures of the earth. One picture-taking session lasted for 21 minutes. Michael Collins explained what was being seen—all of the United States, Canada, Mexico, and Central America.

Then the famous Collins sense of humor took over. He radioed: "Okay, world. Hang onto your hat. I'm going to turn you upside down." And he did—by rolling the camera over on its back.

The men next aimed their cameras at *Columbia*'s interior. Back to earth went pictures of the CSM's food locker and of the astronauts floating about in the weightless atmosphere. They had removed their spacesuits and helmets earlier in the flight and now they could be seen smiling as they moved along the walls and ceiling.

On the second day out, *Columbia* reached the midway point in its journey. For a moment, it stood exactly 120,003 miles from the moon ahead and the earth behind. The third day brought the ship to within 38,000 miles from the moon's surface.

By now, *Columbia* had passed the point where the pull of the moon's gravity became greater than the pull of the earth's gravity. At lift-off, it had reached a speed of 25,000 miles per hour. Then, the earth's pull had gradually slowed it to around 2,000 miles an hour. Now, with the moon tugging hard, *Columbia* began to gain speed again.

Apollo 11 entered its fourth day on Saturday, July 19. The flight was 75 hours and 50 minutes old when the astronauts placed *Columbia* in orbit around the moon. As the spaceship flashed along its course, the three men took television pictures of the lunar surface. Neil Armstrong informed Mission Control that the surface changed color with the changing sunlight. In a full sun, the surface ranged through shades of brown and tan. At dusk, it turned gray.

The time had now come for *Eagle* to play its part. "Buzz" Aldrin crawled through a narrow tunnel in the Command Module, opened a connecting hatch, and climbed into the LM. He quietly checked the ship over. When he spoke, his voice had a happy ring to it. He told Mission Control, "Everything looks beautiful in here." *Eagle* was ready for its trip to the moon's surface.

THE FLIGHT OF *EAGLE*

That flight took place the next day. Aldrin and Armstrong donned their space suits and inched their way into *Eagle,* with Aldrin going first. They sealed themselves in. Then, after giving the instruments a final check, they touched a button.

The LM's spindly legs stretched out from its body and set themselves in their landing position.

Now it was Collins' turn to push a button. The latches that held *Eagle* to *Columbia* popped open. Springs pushed *Eagle* away from the CSM. Armstrong's voice reached Mission Control: "The *Eagle* has wings."

For a short time, *Columbia* and *Eagle* flew side by side in orbit. Then Collins gave *Columbia* a little burst of power. It moved ahead so that *Eagle* would now have room. Armstrong and Aldrin dropped the LM out of orbit and headed for the lunar surface.

With its controls working automatically, *Eagle* spent about two hours dropping to an altitude of 26,000 feet. It was now five miles from its planned landing site—the desolate area known as the Sea of Tranquility. Once *Eagle* landed, Armstrong would christen it and the surrounding lunar surface "Tranquility Base." Armstrong reported to Mission Control that he thought the little ship might overshoot its target.

"THE *EAGLE* HAS LANDED"

Armstrong's voice was calm as he reported the flight's progress. But, suddenly, the instruments in

Mission Control showed that his heart was beginning to race. *Eagle* was now just several hundred feet from the surface. Armstrong's voice was still calm, but his heart was up to 165 beats a minute. What had happened? Why was the astronaut so excited?

The answer: Armstrong saw that the automatic controls were taking the LM into a crater about the size of a football field. The place was strewn with boulders and rocks. They could rip the legs off the little ship if it hit them. And there were smaller craters everywhere. Come down on the side of one of them and *Eagle* would surely tip over. It would then be unable to lift off again. It would be trapped on the lunar surface for all time to come.

Armstrong cut out the automatic pilot. He took over the controls. He guided *Eagle* above the crater while he searched for a clear, flat spot. He saw what he was looking for. Carefully, he headed the LM in for a landing. He brought it down to 60 feet. A worried Mission Control said that there were less than 30 seconds worth of fuel left for the landing.

Armstrong continued to guide the LM toward the level spot. *Eagle* dropped to a height of just 40 feet. Billows of lunar dust sprang up around its spindly legs. At last, there was a slight bump.

Armstrong said, "Houston . . . Tranquility Base here. The *Eagle* has landed."

Mission Control's answer was full of relief: "Roger, Tranquility, we copy you on the ground. You've got a bunch of guys about to turn blue. We're breathing again."

It was 4:18 P.M. Cape Kennedy time. The day was Sunday, July 20, 1969.

FOOTPRINTS ON THE MOON

There was now cheering in Mission Control— and cheering all across the world. An age-old dream had come true. Human beings had done something that had always seemed impossible. They had put two of their kind on the moon.

Eagle was on the moon, yes. But the best was yet to come. Armstrong and Aldrin would now leave the LM. They would actually walk on the lunar surface.

The preparations for that adventure began immediately. Armstrong and Aldrin donned the helmets needed for the walk. They strapped heavy oxygen tanks to their backs. On earth, their equipment had weighed 185 pounds. Here on the moon, it weighed just 30 pounds. But, even though the gear weighed so little, the astronauts had to work slowly. It was very bulky.

At last, the two were ready to go. They opened the LM's hatch. Armstrong was the first to leave the ship. He backed slowly through the hatchway. He took care not to snag his space suit in the narrow opening as he stepped onto a small platform outside the hatchway. He stood there for a moment. Then he started down a ladder.

A television camera was attached to the side of the LM. It clicked on. The world watched as Armstrong stepped down rung by rung. At first, only his boots could be seen. Finally, his whole body came into view. In his white space suit and helmet, he looked like a ghostly creature from space. He was exactly the opposite—a visitor *to* space.

Armstrong reached the circular footpad at the base of one of the LM's legs. He spoke into his helmet microphone and told the world that the LM's footpads had pressed only an inch or so into the lunar surface. Then: "The surface appears to be very, very fine-grained. As you get close to it, it's almost like powder. I'm going to step off the LM now . . ."

He lowered his foot to the dust below. The foot went down slowly, as if he wasn't sure what

he would find there. Then his boot touched the surface. He said: "That's one small step for man, one giant leap for mankind."

Now it was time for Aldrin to leave the LM. Like Armstrong, he backed out through the hatchway. Moments later, he stood at his friend's side. He looked about. His first words were: "Beautiful. Beautiful. Beautiful. A magnificent desolation."

The two astronauts set up a television camera about 30 feet from the LM so that the world could watch all that was happening. Next, Armstrong sent a message to earth. The message was printed on a plaque that was fastened to *Eagle*'s side. He read its words in a quiet voice: "Here man first set foot on the moon, July, 1969. We came in peace for all mankind."

Then the two men brought out an American flag. They fastened it to a pole that they had thrust into the surface. Aldrin inserted a rod into a seam along the upper edge of the flag so that it would stand out straight in the windless air. When the flag was "flying," Aldrin stepped back

Edwin Aldrin, who followed Neil Armstrong and became the second man to stand on the moon, is photographed by Armstrong during his first steps. Armstrong's reflection can be seen in Aldrin's space helmet.

A special camera on the LM took this picture of Neil Armstrong, left, and Edwin Aldrin as they placed the American flag on the surface of the moon.

and saluted. Armstrong stood proudly at attention.

TWO HOURS OF WORK

Armstrong and Aldrin were scheduled to remain outside the LM for a little over two hours. Those hours were to be crowded with various jobs. The astronauts went to work after listening to a radio message of congratulations from President Richard Nixon.

They collected samples of rocks and soil and placed them in bags. They set up a foil screen that was to catch tiny particles of dust carried to the moon by the sun's solar winds. Then they put a seismometer in place. Its job was to record any movements in the moon's crust.

Also put in place was a mirrorlike device. It would reflect laser beams down to earth. The beams would help scientists measure the distance between the moon and the earth with great accuracy. The distance would be measured to an accuracy of six inches.

At one point in their work, Armstrong and Aldrin walked about 300 feet out from the LM. They took motion pictures and still photographs of the surrounding landscape. All the while, they reported details of their life on the moon to Mission Control. Armstrong said the lunar dust looked like powdered charcoal. Aldrin added that it was clinging to his boots and seemed to be sticky. Both men complained that the sunlight was blinding. They had trouble seeing clearly when they moved from the shadows into the light.

A spellbound world watched as the pair moved about. At first, they walked cautiously in the moon's weak gravity. But they became more sure of themselves as the minutes passed. Soon, they seemed to be hopping and leaping along the surface. They looked as if they were having more than a good time. And they were. When Armstrong spoke to Aldrin through his microphone, his voice was full of delight. His words came down to earth: "Isn't this fun?"

High overhead, Michael Collins piloted *Columbia* along its path around the moon. Though his fellow astronauts were right below him, he could not see what they were doing. There was no television receiver aboard the CSM. Before the start of the Apollo journey, he had told Mission Control to make good tapes of the moon walk. He wanted to see them when he got back to earth.

THE WALK ENDS

The minutes flowed past with lightning speed for Armstrong and Aldrin. Their time on the moon grew short. Mission Control ordered them to pack up for the return home. Into large white boxes went the rock and soil samples—and then the foil that had caught the dust in the lunar air. Left in place were the the mirrorlike laser reflector and the seismometer. Scientists would study the information from the two instruments for months to come. Also left in place was the American flag.

The astronauts ended their work by stowing all the boxes aboard *Eagle.* Then they went inside the LM. The hatch swung shut behind them. The moon walk was over.

After watching the astronauts with fascination, the world began to hold its breath. Would *Eagle* now perform as it should? Would the engine in the Ascent Stage work? Would Armstrong and Aldrin get away from the moon? Would the two men return safely to *Columbia*?

All these questions were answered on the mission's sixth day, July 21. *Eagle* performed beautifully. The engine in the Ascent Stage roared when fired. The Lunar Module broke free of its Descent Stage. It was left standing on its spindly legs as the astronauts sped away from the surface. Less than six hours later, the LM joined *Columbia* in orbit. The two ships came together. Armstrong and Aldrin were welcomed aboard the CSM by a grinning Michael Collins.

Eagle was now cut loose from the CSM. It would be left to float in lunar orbit for as long as it could. The astronauts turned *Columbia* toward the earth.

On July 24, after a smooth trip home, *Columbia* splashed down in the South Pacific. Armstrong, Aldrin, and Collins were plucked from the sea by a helicopter and brought to the waiting aircraft carrier, *Hornet.* A short time later, *Columbia* was hoisted aboard the carrier.

The *Apollo 11* mission had taken exactly 8 days, 3 hours, and 19 minutes from launch to splash-down. Its three astronauts had traveled half a million miles. The mission had met President John F. Kennedy's goal of putting a man on the moon by the end of the 1960s. In fact, it had put a man there *before* the end of the 1960s.

It was being called the greatest journey in the history of mankind. It was now at a triumphant end.

7.

THE FIRST STEPS IN A NEW DIRECTION

U.S. moon flights did not end with *Apollo 11.* Six more went out between late 1969 and early 1972. All but one successfully placed astronauts on the lunar surface.

The failed mission was *Apollo 13,* which lifted off in April, 1971. The flight went smoothly until its 55th hour. It was then that the Command/Service Module was rocked by a violent explosion. The shaken astronauts—James Lovell, John Swigert, and Fred Haise—quickly found the reason for the explosion. An electrical problem had caused an oxygen tank on the outside of the Service Module to blow up.

A large section of the Service Module's skin

was torn away. Fortunately, however, the Command Module was undamaged. And the astronauts were unharmed. Had the explosion occurred inside their spaceship, they would have been burned to death—as had been the terrible fate of "Gus" Grissom and his two fellow astronauts back in 1967. They broke the CM away from the battered Service Module.

Despite the accident, the Command Module was still on course. But the scientists in Mission Control were worried. They felt that the CM did not have enough oxygen to get its crew to the moon and back. There was enough oxygen in the capsule for a safe return and a splashdown in the Pacific.

The successful Apollo flights sent their crews down to the lunar surface to explore various areas. Among the regions visited were the Ocean of Storms and Fra Mauro Crater. The last three Apollo flights saw the LM carry a new piece of equipment—the Lunar Roving Vehicle (LRV). This was a small electrically powered car that enabled the astronauts to cover more ground than was possible on foot. The LRV took the astronauts on explorations of up to 20 miles.

Apollo 17, the final moon flight, set an all-time record for a stay on the lunar surface. Eugene

Damage done to Apollo 13 *when an explosion ripped away the outer skin of the Service Module. Moments later the Command Module separated from the SM and the astronauts returned home safely.*

At the far right is the Lunar Roving Vehicle that played a part in the final three Apollo missions to the moon. This photograph was taken during the Apollo 15 *mission.*

Cernan and Harrison H. Schmitt spent four days there. In that time, they made three trips in the LRV, set up equipment that would send information back to earth on the moon's atmosphere, surface, and interior.

A NEW DIRECTION

Though *Apollo 17* ended the moon flights, there were to be three more Apollo missions. Their destination was to be much closer to home. They were to fly up and place their astronauts aboard a giant space laboratory in earth orbit.

The laboratory was known as Skylab. It marked a new direction that the United States was taking in its space work. NASA had long concentrated on manned flights into deep space to see what was to be found there. The new direction now called for the NASA scientists to study space and the planets from space stations floating just miles above the earth.

Skylab was not actually a space station. But it was very much like one. The difference was that a space station is meant to remain aloft indefinitely. Skylab was not designed to last for an indefinite period. (In February, 1986, the Soviets placed the Mir space station in earth orbit. It has been constantly manned by teams of cosmonauts since 1987.)

Scientists hoped to answer a number of questions with Skylab and the men who went up to work in it. They had so far sent astronauts into space for periods of just a few days; now they wanted to know if humans could work in space for weeks and months without falling physically or mentally ill. They also wanted to get an idea of the kinds of scientific tasks that could be performed in space over long time spans.

Skylab took shape while the Gemini and Apollo flights were being launched. When it was completed, it measured 84 feet long and 22 feet wide. Inside were living quarters for three astronauts. Additionally, much space was given to a work area and the equipment it would require. Sitting atop the lab was a telescope. Above it was a set of wings that looked like a windmill. Wings also jutted out from the sides of the ship. All the wings were outfitted with solar panels to collect energy from the sun. The energy would supply the lab with power.

NASA's plans called for three teams of astronauts to occupy Skylab once it was in orbit. The teams would go up one at a time. Each would work in the lab for a certain number of weeks and then be replaced by the next in line. To see how the men fared over long stretches of time, the teams were to work for periods of different lengths. The first would work for a month. The second would spend two months in the lab. The third would remain for three months.

Skylab was the first American space laboratory. But it was not the world's first. The first lab belonged to the Soviet Union. It was a small unit (Skylab was four times bigger) called *Salyut 1* and was launched in 1971. In the next years, the Soviets successfully launched six more Salyut stations. They were visited by various teams of cosmonauts.

SKYLAB IN ORBIT

When Skylab was launched on May 14, 1973, it went into orbit aboard a Saturn rocket. Unfortunately, it was damaged as it hurtled skyward. The damage was caused by a shield that covered the lab and was meant to protect it from the heat. Part of the shield broke loose. It tore off the ship's right wing and damaged the other by jamming it against the hull. The lost wing and the damaged one did not keep the lab from entering orbit. But so many of the solar panels were lost or harmed that the ship's electrical power was sharply reduced.

And so the first three astronauts who went up

to dock with the lab faced a difficult job—the repair of the damaged wing. They were Charles Conrad, Paul Weitz, and scientist Joseph Kerwin. Conrad's time with NASA dated back to the Gemini flights, but Weitz and Kerwin were "space rookies." They were among new groups of astronauts that had been brought into NASA during the late 1960s and the early 1970s.

On reaching Skylab, two of the astronauts floated over to the crippled wing and tried to work it loose from its jammed position. When the job proved impossible, they returned to the CSM, which then docked with Skylab. The astronauts crawled through a hatchway and entered the lab itself. They found the place blazing hot from the sun's rays. This problem was solved by triggering the opening of a large umbrella-like sunshade. As soon as the sunshade, which spread itself out over the top of the lab, began to deflect much of the sun's heat, the interior became cooler.

The astronauts remained in the lab for 29 days. In so doing, they set a record for the longest time spent in space. Until then, two Soviet cosmonauts held the record. They had spent 23 days in a Salyut lab.

During the stay, Conrad and Kerwin ventured outside for another try at repairing the crippled wing. This time, they succeeded in fixing the damage. The job took them three and a half hours. As soon as they were done, the wing's solar panels began to generate electricity.

The next teams to visit Skylab set new time records. The second team remained in the lab for 59 days. During that time, they checked it thoroughly, made a study of solar flares, and took 75,000 photographs of outer space.

The third team put in a stay of 85 days—another new record. As part of their work, the astronauts took photographs of the comet Kohoutek as it passed close to the earth on its 80,000-year orbit around the sun. Kohoutek was said to be far brighter than Halley's comet. But it was so far away that it was barely visible from the lab and showed itself as a mere speck in the photographs.

Feelings were mixed about the Skylab visits when the project was completed. On the one hand, there had been the problem of the damaged wing, plus the headaches of some equipment that didn't work properly. But, on the other hand, the three visits to the lab had netted the NASA scientists a wealth of information about space. In all, the project was considered a success.

Skylab itself remained in orbit until 1979. Still crippled by the damage that had been done during lift-off, the lab began to lose speed and come down out of orbit. It crashed into the earth's atmosphere over Australia and burned to ash and tiny chunks of charred metal.

ANOTHER STEP IN THE NEW DIRECTION

While NASA was working with Skylab, the United States took another "new direction" step in space. The step was taken with the Soviet Union.

The governments of the two countries had spent years distrusting each other because of their differing political views. Each tried to show the world that it was better than the other. As a part of all this, they had raced each other into space. Now both sides wanted to reduce the tension between them and replace it with a beginning friendship. To help matters along, they decided to launch a joint spaceflight. The agreement for sending the flight up was made in 1972 by President Richard M. Nixon and Soviet Premier Alexei Kosygin.

The flight would see an Apollo spacecraft and a Soviet Soyuz spacecraft meet and dock in space, after which the astronauts and cosmonauts would visit each other's ships. The flight itself did not take place until 1975. The two ships were vastly different in many ways and much time was needed to alter them so that they could dock together in space. One major job called for NASA to fit the Apollo's nose with a Docking Module (DM). The DM was a special chamber that would enable the astronauts and cosmonauts to pass from one ship to the other.

Soon after the agreement for the mission had been reached, the Soviets and the Americans announced the names of the men who would make the flight. The Soviets selected Alexei Leonov and Valeri Kubasov. Leonov was the first man ever to walk in space. His walk had taken place back in 1965.

To represent the United States, NASA chose Thomas Stafford, Vance Brand, and Donald "Deke" Slayton. Slayton was one of the original seven astronauts. He had been grounded because of a slight heart problem and had "flown a desk" ever since. He was the only one of the seven never to have flown in space. But now, his problem had eased up enough for him to be sent into space. Everyone at NASA was delighted when he was selected for the mission.

The flight was launched on July 15, 1975. The Soyuz blasted off first. It departed the Soviet

Union in the morning. The Apollo astronauts left 7 hours and 30 minutes later from the Kennedy Space Center. Though the two ships entered orbit on July 15, they did not catch sight of each other until July 17. They began to come together. Down on earth, millions of people watched the drama on television via a camera in the Apollo CSM. The Soyuz was also equipped with a TV camera, but it failed to work at this time.

However, though only the men in the Apollo CSM could be seen, the world was able to hear the voices of both crews on radio. As the two ships touched, the voice of Tom Stafford came down to earth.

He said, "We have capture," meaning that the docking was a success.

Leonov's voice was heard next: "Soyuz and Apollo are shaking hands now."

Stafford answered, "We agree."

The two spacecraft had "shaken hands," yes. But the men themselves did not shake hands until later in the day. Their handshake came after Slayton and Stafford had crawled into the DM and adjusted the air pressure until it matched the pressure in the Soyuz. Then the hatch swung open. Leonov and Kubasov crawled in from the Soyuz. Now hands were clasped. There were

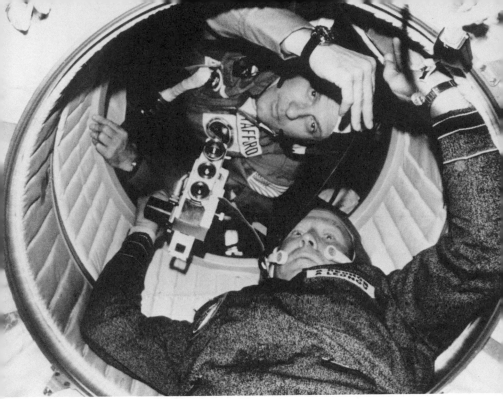

An American-Soviet meeting in space. Astronaut Thomas Stafford takes a look at the Soviet Soyuz spacecraft from the hatchway of the Apollo Docking Module. The cosmonaut is Alexei Leonov.

smiles all around. The men exchanged greetings. The greetings came from President Nixon and Premier Kosygin. Finally, the four spacemen ate lunch together in the DM.

On day two of the meeting, astronauts Brand and Stafford took cosmonaut Kubasov on a tour of the Apollo. Brand then made his way through the DM for a tour of the Soyuz with Kubasov.

Far below on earth, millions of people watched the two visits on television.

The spacemen remained together for four days. Then their ships separated, with each now ready to return to its own country. As the ships moved away from each other, the world below hoped that the visit had helped to pave the way to a greater Soviet-American friendship and understanding.

8.

THE FIRST AMERICAN SPACE SHUTTLES

While the work with Skylab and the U.S.-Soviet flight was going on, NASA took another "new direction" step. It developed the Space Transportation System. The system became known simply as the Shuttle program.

THE SHUTTLE PROGRAM

The program was called the Shuttle because it planned to send spacecraft "shuttling" back and forth between the ground and earth orbit to do a number of jobs. For example, the craft were to carry man-made satellites aloft and place them in

orbit. Ever since the first days of space exploration, both the Americans and the Soviets had
been launching satellites, with the Soviet Union's
Sputnik 1 being the first of the lot. The satellites
were used for a wide variety of purposes. To
mention just two of their jobs, they gathered information for weather forecasts and made studies
of space and the earth.

The program was also to send up spacecraft to
make repairs on existing satellites. In addition, the
ships could bring damaged satellites back to earth
for repair if they could not be fixed in space. A
major job would see the Shuttles carry supplies
and equipment to space stations.

The Mercury, Gemini, and Apollo capsules had
all been built to be used just one time. But it
would be too costly to build a new shuttle craft
for each new trip into space. And so NASA set
about designing a craft that could be used again
and again. What was finally developed was a ship
that consisted of two parts. One part was the Orbiting Vehicle (OV). The other part was the External Tank (ET).

THE ORBITING VEHICLE

The OV was so named because it was the main
part of the shuttle that would carry astronauts in

orbit. It looked very much like an airplane because it was fitted with wings and had a tail assembly. The ship measured 122 feet long and had a wingspan of 78 feet. It was covered over with ceramic tiles to protect it from the heat that came with lift-off and the later return to the earth's atmosphere.

Located up in its nose was the flight deck, where two pilots controlled the ship. Below and behind the deck were living and work quarters for the crew. Then came the cargo bay, where the material being carried into space would be stored. The bay measured 60 feet long and 15 feet wide. It was fitted with giant overhead doors. They were kept closed until the time came to unload the bay.

The tail section contained the OV's main rocket engine. The main engine was to be used to help get the Shuttle off the ground. There were also smaller maneuvering engines. These would be used to change direction while in orbit. They would also be used to slow the craft down when it was ready to leave orbit and return to earth.

Though the OV could be handled by two astronauts, it had room to carry a crew of seven. The five additional astronauts were to be technicians who would do whatever work was needed while in space.

THE EXTERNAL TANK

The External Tank carried the rocket fuel needed to thrust the OV into space. Looking like a gigantic barrel with a stubby nose, the ET measured 154 feet long and 28 feet wide. The OV rode piggyback on the External Tank when heading into space.

Attached to the sides of the tank were two rockets, called boosters. They helped to lift the entire Shuttle off the ground.

THE SHUTTLE IN FLIGHT

At the start of a flight, the OV's main engine and the booster rockets provided the power for lift-off. The booster rockets burned for about two minutes into the flight. Once their fuel was gone, they were released. They fell into the Atlantic and were picked up by a waiting ship so that they could be used again. They did not burn up on the way to the ocean because the OV had not yet broken out of the earth's atmosphere.

After the boosters had been dropped off, the External Tank continued to provide the OV with fuel and carried the ship almost to orbital height. Then, when its fuel supply was exhausted, it, too, was released. It fell away, struck the earth's atmosphere, and burned to ash.

The OV moved into orbit. Once there, its crew went about their work. When they had finished, the OV fired its smaller engines, left orbit, and entered the earth's atmosphere. Then it became a giant glider. Without using engine power, it floated gracefully to earth. Because it was equipped with wheels, it landed on the ground rather than in the ocean.

THE FIRST SHUTTLE FLIGHTS

The first Space Shuttle was ready in 1977. Christened *Enterprise,* it was to be used for testing only, to see if any more work was needed before the Shuttle system was tried in space. The ship went through its tests at Edwards Air Force Base in California. It did not travel into orbit. Nor did it travel atop the External Tank. Instead, it rode piggyback on a Boeing 747 airliner.

The OV made its first test flight on August 12, 1977. It was carried skyward on the 747 and then released. The OV swept upward and began to move along on its own. The two-man crew flew it for a short time and then brought it in for a graceful landing. They were elated. They said that the OV had been easy to handle.

Enterprise made four test flights. It passed them all with flying colors. NASA felt certain that the Shuttle system could now be safely tried in orbit. The first orbital flight, however, was not assigned to *Enterprise.* It had been meant only for testing and it had done its job. Another OV—named *Columbia*—was put in place at the Kennedy Space Center. It looked like a strange giant as it sat piggyback on the External Tank and awaited launch day.

That day came on April 12, 1981. *Columbia*'s main engine and the booster rockets thundered to life. The monster shot into the air. The booster rockets fell away on schedule, followed a few minutes later by the ET. *Columbia,* with John Young and Robert Crippen at its controls, went into orbit. It remained there for 54 hours and 21 minutes.

The two pilots brought the ship down through

The Space Shuttle Discovery *glides in for a successful landing after three days in orbit in 1985.*

the earth's atmosphere on April 14. They glided in for a landing at Edwards Air Force Base. Except for one slight problem, the flight had been a complete success. Some of the protective tiles on the OV's outer skin had broken away during the mission.

The flight marked a new first for NASA. *Columbia* was the first American craft to leave the earth's atmosphere and then return to land on the ground rather than in the water. And the flight marked a personal first for astronaut John Young. He was the first American to fly in space five times.

THE SHUTTLE AT WORK

In the next years, NASA launched more than twenty Shuttle missions. *Columbia* did not fly them all. The ship was joined by three others—*Challenger, Discovery,* and *Atlantis. Challenger* made its

first flight in 1983. *Discovery* followed in 1984, and *Atlantis* in 1985.

The ships, which carried crews ranging in number from two to seven, performed a wide variety of tasks during those years. They placed communications satellites in orbit. They made repairs of existing satellites. They tested tools and other equipment designed for use in space.

The flights also gave NASA a new series of space firsts. A *Challenger* flight in 1983 carried the first American woman to visit space—Sally Ride. She was the world's third woman in space. The first was the Soviet Union's Valentina Tereshkova, who had traveled into orbit in 1963. The second woman also came from the Soviet Union. She was Svetlana Savitsky. Her space flight was made in 1982.

Sally Ride, a physicist, was among the ever-growing number of astronauts recruited by NASA. The newcomers included several women, among them Judith Resnik, who became the second American woman in space. Sally Ride went on to win the honor of being the first American woman to visit space twice.

Another first for NASA was scored by *Challenger* a little later in 1983. The ship took Guion Bluford, Jr., into orbit. He became the first black astronaut to travel in space.

Sally Ride, the first American woman in space.

Guion Bluford was the first black astronaut to travel in space.

The Shuttle missions went so well that NASA began saying that shuttles would be launched on a regular basis by the late 1980s. By then, NASA expected to be sending up twenty-five flights a year. But then disaster struck.

A TERRIBLE DAY IN JANUARY

January 26, 1986, dawned bright and clear at Cape Canaveral. *Challenger* stood gleaming on its pad, ready to lift off on the Shuttle program's twenty-fifth flight. It was to carry aloft a giant communications satellite—called the Tracking and Data Relay Satellite (TDRS)—and send it into orbit around the globe. Built at a cost of $100 million, the TDRS would relay information from other satellites to earth.

Weighing more than 5,000 pounds, the TDRS lay locked in the cargo bay as *Challenger* awaited the moment of blast-off. Up on the flight deck, seven crew members sat strapped in their seats and ready to go. The seven were:

FRANCIS "DICK" SCOBEE, flight commander
RONALD McNAIR
ELLISON ONIZUKA
JUDITH RESNIK
MICHAEL SMITH

GREGORY JARVIS
SHARON CHRISTA MCAULIFFE

Of the seven, Christa McAuliffe was the one best known to the public. Her name had been in the news for weeks. She was the first person chosen to take part in NASA's new Space Participant Program. The program hoped to educate the public about space by taking private citizens on flights. At the request of President Ronald Reagan, the first person chosen had come from the ranks of the country's teachers. Christa had won the honor over 11,146 fellow teachers.

She was age 37 and taught social studies in a New Hampshire high school. After traveling into orbit, she was to tell students everywhere of her experiences and of the science of space and space flight.

As usual, countless Americans—including pupils in classrooms across the nation—were in front of their TV sets to watch *Challenger* lift off. Present at Cape Canaveral were the throngs that always gathered at flight time. Members of the McAuliffe family were among the NASA guests at the Kennedy Space Center.

The launch took place at 11:38 A.M. It went perfectly. *Challenger,* gathering speed every second, headed skyward. By the time it reached an altitude of 47,000 feet, the ship was traveling 1,800 feet per second. It was then that a small flame broke out and brought disaster. The flame erupted on the rocket booster on the External Tank's right side. Fifteen seconds after it first appeared, there was a tremendous explosion as the ET's half-million gallons of fuel blew up.

The External Tank was torn apart. A giant fireball filled the sky. *Challenger* and its TDRS cargo disappeared within it and were blown to pieces. The two booster rockets were ripped from the ET and went zigzagging crazily through the air.

Far below, there was horror across the watching nation. No one was certain what had happened. But everyone knew that something had gone terribly wrong.

Then came the awful news that just 73 seconds into its flight, *Challenger* had met its death because of a leak in the right booster rocket. Volatile fuel had seeped out into the air and had caught fire. A later investigation showed that the leak had taken shape when an O-ring had failed. Its job was to help keep the fuel sealed within the booster.

Seven people had died instantly with their ship. Their deaths marked the greatest loss of life suf-

Crew members who lost their lives when **Challenger***'s External Tank exploded just seconds after lift-off. Front row, left to right: Michael Smith, Francis Scobee, Ronald McNair. Back row, left to right: Ellison Onizuka, Christa McAuliffe, Gregory Jarvis, Judith Resnik.*

fered in the history of United States space exploration.

STARTING OVER

The accident caused NASA to cancel plans for the next Shuttle launches. Space scientists and engineers spent the next months studying the reasons for the disaster and developing methods that would make future flights safer. During those months, Americans everywhere thought that their country might end its manned space flights for all time to come.

But, though deeply saddened, many people soon realized that manned flight would not end but would begin anew one day soon. They understood that all exploration has been achieved at a terrible cost in human life. Throughout history, they said, thousands of land and ocean explorers had lost their lives as they attempted to learn more about our world. The same held true for the first men and women who took off in their fragile airplanes to explore the wonders of flight and to map out the routes that are today used by the airlines of every nation. And the same was to hold true if space was to be fully explored.

They were right. In early 1988, NASA announced its plans to restart the Shuttle program. Those plans called for *Discovery* to embark on a four-day flight in August or September of the year. One of its main jobs would be to place a new Tracking and Data Relay Satellite in orbit around the earth. It was a duplicate of the TDRS that had been aboard on *Challenger*'s last flight.

Five astronauts were chosen for the flight. They were:

RICHARD COVEY, Air Force officer
FREDERICK HAUCK, Navy officer
JOHN "MIKE" LOUNGE, former Navy pilot
DAVID HILMERS, Marine Corps flier
GEORGE "PINKY" NELSON, astronomer

Frederick Hauck was named commander of the group. To Richard Covey went the job of *Discovery*'s pilot. They and their three companions were all veteran astronauts. All had flown on earlier Shuttle missions. And all, with *Challenger*'s death sharply etched in their memories, knew that they faced great danger when they blasted off. But they were ready for whatever the future held. David Hilmers expressed the feelings of the five men when he told news reporters that everyone must face danger at one time or another in life. He said that he was ready to risk his life on the flight because the *Discovery* mission was of such great importance to the future of U.S. space work.

The scheduling of the mission came after *Discovery* was given a major overhaul. The ship's flight systems underwent some 400 changes. Improvements were made in its main engines and steering system. The booster rockets were redesigned to avoid the leak that had led to *Challenger's* destruction.

NASA worked slowly and carefully on the coming flight. In the past, it had moved swiftly in planning and dispatching Shuttle flights. Many people felt that the swiftness had been much responsible for the *Challenger* tragedy. Now NASA had just one thought in mind—to get the nation back into space but to do so as safely as possible. Safety demanded that the work be done at a snail's pace, with all changes and improvements in the Shuttle being checked and rechecked before being approved.

The astronauts went through a rigorous training program. Using a mock-up of *Discovery*, they rehearsed the flight out from earth and then practiced the work that would be done when the time came to release the 5,000-pound TDRS from the ship's cargo bay. A major part of their training was devoted to handling any problem that might crop up during the mission. About 95 percent of their training was spent practicing what to do in all sorts of possible emergencies.

In early July, 1988, *Discovery* was taken to the Vehicle Assembly Building at the Kennedy Space Center. There, it was attached to the External Tank and the booster rockets. Then, riding atop a giant crawler-transporter, it traveled out to its launch site—Pad 39-B. The trip to the pad covered four miles and took seven hours to complete.

Once at the launch site, *Discovery* underwent two tests before being cleared for lift-off. Its main engines were test-fired, followed by a firing of the redesigned booster rockets. Though there were delays along the way due to technical problems, both tests were successfully completed. NASA scientists and engineers cleared *Discovery* for blast-off on September 29, 1988—more than two and a half years after the *Challenger* flight had ended in tragedy.

INTO SPACE WITH *DISCOVERY*

The sky above Cape Canaveral was bright and painted with clouds at 9:30 in the morning. The roads, beaches, and open lands around the Kennedy Space Center were crowded with more than a million people, all with their eyes turned toward the distant Pad 39-B. Throughout the nation, millions more sat in front of their television sets and stared at the gleaming white *Discovery* as it clung to the back of the giant External Tank.

All the spectators at the Cape and at home shared two emotions—hope and dread. They hoped that *Discovery* would blast off safely in the next few moments and mark the rebirth of America's work in space. But they dreaded that something might go wrong, just as it had gone so wrong on that awful day back in 1986.

The suspense lasted longer than anyone had expected. There was a delay because of weather conditions. Winds high above were not ideal for *Discovery*'s launch. NASA, being cautious again, waited until they felt sure that all would be well. Then the moment came at 11:37 A.M. Everyone held their breaths as flames burst from beneath *Discovery*. Smoke billowed across Pad 39-B. A thunderous roar spread out in all directions. *Discovery* trembled and then climbed slowly into the air. It gained speed as it moved higher and cut a path out over the Atlantic Ocean. There were cheers from the watchers. But they came from throats tight with fear.

For more than a minute, everyone watched tensely. Only when *Discovery* had shot through the 73rd second of its flight did the watchers begin to relax. It was at that 73-second mark that the shining *Challenger* had dissolved into a terrible ball of fire.

The sense of relaxation turned to jubilation as the next moments passed. At about two minutes into the flight, *Discovery*'s booster rockets finished their work and were set free for the drop back down to the Atlantic. The External Tank fell away 6½ minutes later. Then, at the end of another half hour, *Discovery* went into orbit. The ship and its five astronauts were now some 180 miles above the earth.

The jubilation and the deep feeling of relief grew as *Discovery* flew through its beginning orbits. During the fifth orbit, the crew turned to the first of their mission assignments—deployment of the TDRS satellite. Once it was out of the cargo bay, controls moved it away from the Obiter. Attached rockets then sent it to a height of 22,300 feet and into earth orbit above the equator. The TDRS will be a critical link in a communications network for future spacecraft.

OTHER ASSIGNMENTS

With the TDRS safely launched, the *Discovery* astronauts turned to other assignments. They devoted the next days to a series of scientific experiments. One experiment saw them study the effects of weightlessness on complex mixtures of chemicals. Another looked at the effects of weightlessness on the growth of inorganic substances. Still another tried to learn what weightlessness could do to help form large crystal grains that could be used to strengthen certain metal alloys.

All the while, the five men tested and checked the workings of *Discovery*'s new and improved flight systems. At one point, they aimed cameras at the earth's horizon, taking photographs that would contribute to a study of the atmosphere at sunrise and sunset. At another point, they paused to send down to earth messages honoring the seven astronauts who had died aboard *Challenger.*

All five men spoke of the lost seven. One of the most touching statements came from mission commander Frederick Hauck. He said: "Today, up here where the blue sky turns to black, we can say at long last, to Dick, Mike, Judy, to Ron and El, and to Christa and Greg: Dear friends, we have resumed the journey that we promised to continue for you; dear friends, your loss has meant that we could confidently begin anew; dear friends, your spirit and your dream are still alive in our hearts."

THE MISSION ENDS

Discovery was in its 64th orbit of the earth when the time came to end the mission. The crew turned the giant ship so that it was flying tail-first. They then fired two rockets that slowed the craft. The firing took place while they were 185 miles above the Indian Ocean and close to the east coast of Africa. Lasting 2 minutes and 50 seconds, it caused the ship to begin descending along a path that would carry the astronauts half-way around the world to their landing site.

That landing site was Edwards Air Force Base in southern California. Hours before dawn on October 3, 1988, people began gathering in the barren desert around the base to watch *Discovery*'s return to earth. By the time the Shuttle came into view as a mere speck in the sky, some 425,000 sightseers were on hand. Their cars choked all the roads leading to the base.

The journey back down into the earth's atmosphere went smoothly, except for one problem. The cooling system in *Discovery*'s main cabin, which had failed for a short time just after lift-off, now went out again and promised to cause the astronauts and their electronic gear trouble as they sped through the heat generated by the thickening air. But, for some unknown reason, it came back to life within a few minutes.

Just after 9:30 A.M., *Discovery* swept over Edwards Air Force Base. Then it banked sharply to the left and came around for its final approach. Traveling at about 250 miles an hour—100 mph faster than commercial airliners when landing— the ship dropped toward the runway at the rate of 180 feet per second. Its angle of descent was 19 percent. Then it leveled off for touchdown. The wheels touched the runway.

It was exactly 9:37 A.M. *Discovery* and its five astronauts were safely home. They had orbited the earth 64 times and had come down on the 65th orbit. The four-day mission had carried them through space for a distance of 1.68 million miles.

Discovery's flight was deemed a complete success. Americans everywhere knew that their country had recovered from a terrible tragedy. The United States had returned to space and to all the work that is to be done there. With that return and with the missions now being planned by NASA, we can expect that the future will soon bring us great new "firsts" in manned space flight—either in earth orbit or in the vast reaches beyond.

RECOMMENDED READING LIST

If you would like to read more about space exploration and space travel, you will find the following books to be of great interest and value. You should be able to find them in your public or school library.

Barbour, John, and the Writers and Editors of The Associated Press. *Footprints on the Moon.* New York: The Associated Press, 1969.

Bendik, Jeanne. *Space Travel.* New York: Franklin Watts, Inc., 1982.

Berger, Melvin. *Space Shots, Shuttles and Satellites.* New York: G. P. Putnam's Sons, 1983.

Billings, Charlene W. *Christa McAuliffe, Pioneer Space Teacher.* Hillside, New Jersey: Enslow Publishers, 1986.

Branley, Franklyn M. *From Sputnik to Space Shuttles: Into*

the New Space Age. New York: Thomas Y. Crowell, 1986.

———— *Experiments in the Principles of Space Travel* (revised). New York: Thomas Y. Crowell, 1973.

Collins, Michael. *Flying to the Moon and Other Strange Places.* New York: Farrar, Straus and Giroux, 1976.

Coombs, Charles. *Passage to Space: The Shuttle Transportation System.* New York: William Morrow and Company, 1979.

———— *Skylab.* New York: William Morrow and Company, 1972.

Dwiggins, Don. *Flying the Space Shuttles.* New York: Dodd, Mead & Company, 1985.

Farmer, Gene, and Hamblin, Dora Jane. *First on the Moon: A Voyage with Neil Armstrong, Michael Collins, Edwin E. Aldrin, Jr.* Boston: Little, Brown and Company, 1970.

Fuchs, Erich. *Journey to the Moon.* New York: Delacorte Press, 1969.

Gurney, Gene. *Walk in Space: The Story of Project Gemini.* New York: Random House, 1967.

Hawkes, Nigel. *Space Shuttle.* New York: Gloucester Press, 1983.

Holder, William G. *Saturn V: The Moon Rocket.* New York: Julian Messner, 1970.

Kerrod, Robin. *Race for the Moon.* Minneapolis: Lerner Publications, 1980.

Stine, G. Harry. *Shuttle into Space: A Ride in America's Space Transportation System.* Chicago: Follett Publishing, 1972.

Yenne, Bill. *The Astronauts: The First 25 Years of Manned Space Flight.* New York and Connecticut: Exeter Books and Bison Books, 1986.

INDEX